OF WITCHES AND RUIN

JULIE CALDWELL

ISBN: 979-8-9880180-0-1 (Paperback)

ISBN: 979-8-9880180-1-8 (Ebook)

Book Cover by MiblArt

1st edition 2023

To the teachers who helped shape my life

CHAPTER ONE

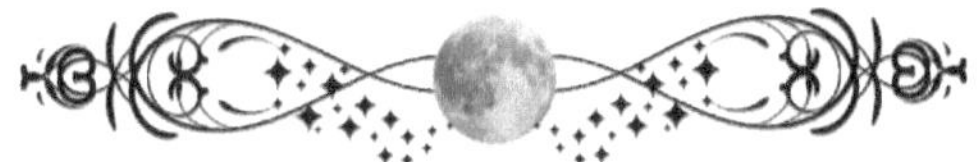

I'VE EXPERIENCED HELL BEFORE. High school was so much worse. I sat in class, learning about the insignificant town of Salem, Massachusetts, when I peered to my right and saw Richelle—the classic mean girl—try to put gum in some blonde nerd's hair. I sighed. Amateur. If I were her—and had I been at my old school—I would have dropped an Ice Lizard down her blouse to let her experience what frostbite really was.

But I was no longer the mean girl. My friends had reformed me. With a flitting glance to establish no one was paying attention, I held my palm under the desk and directed it at her backpack. Okay, they *mostly* reformed me.

"*Ignis,*" I whispered.

I bit my full lip to suppress a grin as I saw flames burst from the pink nylon. My best friend, Melissa McFadden, ever ready to provide a helping hand, was the first to notice. She sprinted to Richelle's side and tapped out the fire. The class erupted into hysterics while I tried to contain my amusement. I failed.

The teacher called for order, but no one was listening. She threw her hands up in defeat and dismissed the class early. She sent Richelle to the office to calm down, and she sent me there for laughing at Richelle's distress.

I gathered my stuff and strolled out of the classroom with everybody else. At least the nerd's hair remained untouched, and I temporarily satisfied my boredom. Melissa bounded up to me, her curly golden blonde hair bouncing, a total contrast to my brown and pastel pink hair, and linked her arm through mine. She threw me a stern look.

"What?" I asked, all too innocent.

"You shouldn't have laughed. What if that happened to your backpack?"

"If it were my backpack, I would have made s'mores in the ashes of my homework."

Melissa let out a spontaneous giggle. "And you probably would have blamed it on magic or something."

I stiffened. "Magic isn't real."

Melissa didn't know I was a witch. No one did. If anyone found out, it would spell disaster for my entire race and every other race in the realm. No pun intended.

"Of course it's not," Melissa said, rolling her eyes. "But you would use any excuse to not do schoolwork."

I tried to chuckle, but it came out as a weird coughing noise. Melissa looked at me confused. I shook my head and turned my lips upward in what I hoped was a reassuring smile.

We were in front of the principal's office now. I gave her an overdramatic salute as I headed in to face my judgment.

The office of Principal Paladina was as generic as any other school administrator's office. The walls were beige, and abstract art hung everywhere. Honestly, it looked more like a hospital room than a principal's office. Except for the enormous mahogany desk in the middle.

Mr. Paladina was sitting behind that desk, and in one of the two chairs in front sat Richelle. Her eyes were blotchy, no doubt from crying about her designer backpack going up in smoke. Mr. Paladina motioned for me to sit down in the empty chair. I plopped into it and gave the principal an award-winning smile.

"You know why you're here, right?" he asked.

"Actually no," I said. "The teacher said I was a shining example to the student body."

Paladina raised an eyebrow. I was hedging my bets by giving him sass, but I couldn't help it. Humans were fun to play with.

"You set my backpack on fire!" Richelle screeched from where she was sitting.

"If I had done it, I would have set you on fire."

"Miss Amberwood!" Principal Paladina yelled.

I sagged my shoulders, hoping I looked regretful. Maybe I shouldn't have said that. I didn't need to get expelled before the banishment from my world ended.

After half an hour of lectures from Paladina, Richelle accusing me of setting her things on fire again (with no proof), and a conversation with the guidance counselor about how "laughing while a student is suffering" is a cry for help, I was off to my next class.

Unfortunately, my next class was with Richelle. We walked together silently into the art room and she gave me a dirty glare as I walked by her. I smiled at her as I took my seat at the easel. Acrylic paint in various colors sat in front of me. I dipped my brush into the black and drew a middle finger with Richelle's name on it. Richelle turned red when she saw what I had painted. Instead of ratting me out, she actually flipped me the bird.

When class was almost over and I had a decent painting done, Richelle walked over to my easel with a tub of neon pink paint, and dumped it all over my work.

"Sorry," Richelle said, "I didn't see your hideous drawing behind my paint."

I wanted to incinerate her right there. Instead, I took a deep breath, smiled, and picked up the canvas. I shoved my way past her, smearing a mix of the pink paint and the neutral tones underneath all over Richelle's clothes.

"You bitch!" she yelled, loud enough for the teacher to come over and ask what the problem was.

"She spilled paint all over my clothes!" Richelle cried.

"You poured paint all over my canvas!"

"Ladies! Enough," he said. "Both of you will have plenty of time to communicate during detention. Right now, clean this mess up. And Richelle, find some other clothes in the office." He walked back to the front of the classroom, shaking his head.

Richelle shot me the biggest death glare she could, and I smirked uncontrollably. So I had detention. At least I could catch up on some sleep.

Detention was more like community service. Paladina ordered Richelle and me to clean the cafeteria. We had to wipe down the tables, mop the floor, and get used gum off the tables and chairs. So much for sleeping on the job.

I had a spray bottle full of cleaner in one hand, and a rag in the other. I was methodically wiping down the tables when Richelle's phone rang. She stopped mopping the floor and answered the call.

"Yes." The clipped tone of her voice made my ears perk up. Almost as if she was afraid. "No... I'll be there as soon as I can... no, I can still do this... Yes sir, I'm on my way now."

She hung up the phone and dragged the mop bucket over to me.

"I have to bail. Be a darling and finish my chores, won't you?"

"Why? Daddy's not going to buy you a Mercedes if you don't come home right now?" I asked.

"It's none of your business, freak." She pushed past me, and in her hurry, she tripped over the bucket and dumped dirty water all over the floor. And me.

"Why you little—" I wanted to turn her into the slug she was, but there was a difference between causing a little mayhem and changing someone's existence. I wasn't cruel enough to do that.

She brushed herself off and flipped her brunette hair over her shoulder as she walked out the front entrance, leaving me to clean the cafeteria alone.

When I got home, I raced upstairs and set my non-charcoaled backpack on the floor and heaved myself onto the bed.

A few minutes later, a knock at the door informed me that my aunt was home. I sat up and grumbled for her to come in.

She entered and paced around the middle of the room for a long time before I asked her what was wrong.

"You used magic and got detention? On the same day?"

I huffed. "How did you find out?"

"The school called me. You set a girl's backpack on fire?"

"No one got hurt," I said.

My aunt pursed her full lips and tightened her eyes, making her look like the adult my parents expected her to be. She called this her "impostor mom" look. Most of the time, she looked like she needed to use the bathroom. Not today. Today she looked like my mother. Not a good sign.

"Ebony, you have to be discreet." she said, "There's a lot of cruel history between Salem and witches. People are still suspicious."

"A fact that you have drilled into my brain every day since I got here."

I knew about the history between my people and the humans. Witches and humans used to live among each other, albeit the humans had no clue their neighbors were practicing magic. A few witches, however, got overconfident and started practicing out in the open. Humans took notice. They grew afraid and paranoid. Scared to the point of putting their own kind to death. Witches grew afraid too—afraid of exposure. So the King of Amethystia, my home, ordered every witch living in the human world back to the realm. Very few witches have left since.

My aunt sat on the edge of my bed. She placed her calloused hands on her knees, a gesture she did when she was uncomfortable. She hated doing the parenting thing. I hated being lectured. It was a lose-lose for everybody involved.

"We were lucky no one got hurt," she said.

"Well, I think I scared Richelle pretty good."

Aunt Jasmine raised her eyebrows and held out her palm. "No phone for three days."

My head fell back as I groaned. The cell phone was one of the good things about this realm! I reluctantly gave it over, however, and her body loosened. Parenting mode was over.

Half an hour later, I was in the living room watching Aunt Jasmine finish one of her paintings when the doorbell rang. We made our way over to the door, even though we both already knew who it was.

Sam Freeman, my other best friend, was standing on the porch, ready to tutor me. With his sun-kissed skin and coiffed brown hair, he was ready to be featured in an edition of *GQ*. It didn't help that he had broad shoulders and muscles that were lean yet defined.

I was failing about three of my classes and Sam, being ever helpful, volunteered himself to make sure I didn't flunk out. I assumed he was joking at first, but when he appeared at our door every day for a week straight, I just resigned myself to more studying.

Sam went into the kitchen and put his stuff down on the table. He pulled out two calculators.

"I thought we could get started on some equations that are going to be on the midterms." he said.

A groan came from my throat. And here I thought my phone getting taken away was the worst thing that would happen today.

Sam and I had been working on the same problem for fifteen minutes when I flung the book across the room.

"I don't get it!"

Sam's brow furrowed while his lips puckered. That meant he was thinking. After a few minutes, I saw a lightbulb come on in his head. He grabbed the book from the floor and we went over the equation differently. While the new way Sam taught me clicked, my brain had had enough.

I was about to say screw it on the no magic in front of human rule and thrust a fireball at the textbook when my aunt walked into the kitchen. The last thing I needed was another witness to watch me suffer, but she proposed we put the books aside for the night. A sigh escaped my lips and all the tension from the last few hours left my body. Sam let out a small chuckle. My mouth pulled into a grimace and in return, Sam stuck his tongue out at me.

Sam's mom called him home early, so I was at the kitchen table, looking at the increasingly fuzzy numbers swimming in my head. Being too stubborn to quit, I read equations and formulas until well after midnight.

The next morning, I woke up to the smell of freshly brewed coffee. I lifted my head and my neck twinged a bit. I looked at my surroundings and realized I fell asleep at the kitchen table.

"Good morning!" Aunt Jasmine said in a singsong tone.

The only response I could mutter was a groan.

"I have coffee for you. Dark roast. You look like you need it."

"Why didn't you wake me last night?" My voice was hoarse.

"And get a blast of magic to the face? No, thank you. I learned early on never to wake you unless absolutely necessary."

I nodded as I took the mug of dark liquid. Smart woman.

I went up to my room, cursing the fact that I'm a heavy sleeper, and got dressed for school. I put on my favorite maroon jacket, headed downstairs and out the door.

Melissa ambushed me with a hug as I was putting my books into my locker.

"Ahh!" I yelled as the pain in my neck spasmed.

"What's up?" Melissa let go and looked me up and down.

"Slept wrong."

Melissa's face relaxed, and she smiled. "I have just the thing for that!"

She dug into her baby blue backpack and pulled out a bottle of Tylenol.

I took two, grateful that I wouldn't have to be in pain much longer, though carrying Tylenol was against school policy. Melissa and I made our way to our first class, and she sat down beside me.

While the teacher was lecturing us about the history of the human realm, Melissa passed me a note.

Why didn't you text me back last night?

I scribbled down my answer. I looked up at the teacher, making sure her back was turned and passed the note back.

Aunt Jasmine took my phone.

Melissa looked up at me in shock. She then bent down and furiously scribbled something else. She passed the note back to me.

That's cruel and unusual punishment. You should sue.

I bit back a laugh. As I was about to pass my answer back to her, Ms. Lewis chose that moment to call on me for an answer to a question I didn't hear.

"Um... yes?"

"I'm so glad you agree with me, Miss Amberwood." she said. "Now tell me, in what year did the British exile Napoleon?"

I didn't have an answer, so I shrunk back in my desk and shrugged.

"Well, I suspect you would have known the answer if you and Miss McFadden weren't passing notes."

The class snickered while Melissa and I looked at each other in embarrassment.

Sam met up with us after class, beaming because he got an A-plus on his English exam.

Melissa and I rolled our eyes, and we made our way down the hall.

Halfway to my next class, I felt a sudden jolt of electricity pass through me. It took the breath out of my lungs. I fell to the floor, unable to process what was happening. Another shot of electricity went through me, and I knew I had to get home. I didn't know why I had to get there, but I knew it was important. Why couldn't I breathe? I got shakily to my feet, ignoring the worried shouts of my friends, and sprinted to the house.

CHAPTER TWO

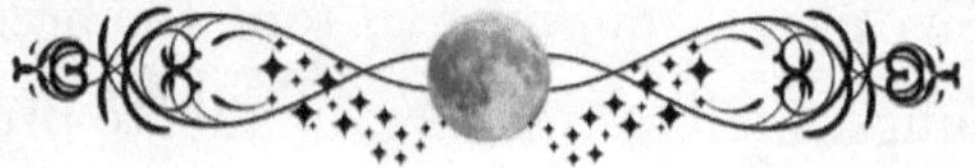

I SENT A SILENT thank you to Hecate when I arrived at the edge of the cul-de-sac and saw my aunt's off-white colonial home still standing. I bounded up the porch steps and pulled out my key to the front door. Except there was no door to put the key into. Someone had forced it off its hinges.

Carefully, I walked through the entryway and jerked to a stop in what used to be the living room. Now, it was a jumble of couch fluff and torn books. My face fell slack as I wandered further into the house. The television was still on the wall, but someone smashed the screen in.

I heard rustling behind me, and I gasped as I whirled toward the sound. With an energy ball invoked, I tip-toed to the kitchen, taking care not to make a sound. Drawing in a deep breath, I bounded around the corner with a battle cry as I heaved the globe of electricity from my palm.

A high-pitched screech came from the origin of the rustling, and a black and white spotted cat that had strayed in went nuts and rushed out the open back door. Smoke curled upward from the scorch mark left on the wall beside the doorway and I grimaced. Aunt Jasmine probably wouldn't notice with all the other damage.

Once my pulse had slowed, I took in my surroundings. The bright white kitchen, like the living room, was in shambles. Pots and pans had been strewn everywhere, and someone had rummaged through the drawers flinging knives and silverware every which way. On my way upstairs, I noticed the intruder shattered the pictures of my aunt and her friends. I got to the top of the stairs and halted. The intruder had kicked in every door. Even the one to the bathroom. I dashed to my room and found pieces of glass littering the floor around the splintered mirror. Whoever had been here destroyed my bed and split open the mattress. Fluff from the torn pillows covered the carpet, making it look like it had snowed, and my closet was a tangle of loose clothes.

I forced myself to investigate the other rooms. All of them wrecked, but nothing of value was missing. Or at least, nothing I could see. I heard the wood of the front door rattle downstairs. My body went rigid. Closing my eyes, I drew in an unsteady breath and strode to the top landing. I noticed a shadow approach, and out of instinct, my arm shot out in front of me.

"*Magicae!*" I shouted as I sent a pulse of pure purple magic toward whoever was in the house.

"*Subsistio!*" I heard someone yell from below, and the blast of magic dissipated before reaching its target.

"Aunt Jasmine?" I staggered down the stairs.

"Ebony," she said with obvious relief. "Are you alright?"

"I think so. I was at school and something like a rush of energy shot through me. Somehow, I knew something was wrong here. So I rushed home and found it like this."

"That jolt you received was the barrier around the house being broken. Think of it as a security system, but instead of the alarm alerting the authorities, it alerts us," Aunt Jasmine said.

I tried to nod, but all I could manage was a frightened shake.

Aunt Jasmine wrapped me in a hug and squeezed tight.

"Who did this?" I asked, my voice muffled by her shoulder.

"I don't know, but whoever was here was searching for something."

"Searching for what?" I asked.

"The Amberwood family is ancient and powerful. We have a collection of artifacts and spells passed down through the generations. And our political position means we have an abundance of enemies."

I pulled out of the hug. Of course, this was about our family.

Aunt Jasmine gave me a compassionate glance. She didn't like our family much either. There was a reason she changed her last name back to Evenfell.

We took one last peek around the house to make sure there were no traps set by the intruder. We got to cleaning, keeping our eyes out for anything missing as we went.

The sun was disappearing behind the horizon when we heard footsteps approach. Aunt Jasmine swore and told me to stay put as she grabbed a poker from the fireplace and walked toward the front door. I didn't listen and followed behind to make sure whoever was here wouldn't try anything. Sam and Melissa stood on the porch, straining to glimpse the chaos behind the entryway. Aunt Jasmine blocked their view as best she could. I ducked under her arm and greeted my friends, hoping they couldn't hear the tremble in my voice.

"Hey guys. What's up?"

"You... You don't have a door," Sam said shellshocked.

"Sure we do!" I pointed to the broken wood laying on the ground. "It's right there."

"What happened?" Melissa asked. The setting sun shone on her tanned skin and brightened her deep blue eyes. Eyes that were full of concern and bewilderment. I glanced at Sam and his caramel-colored eyes were also full of anxiety. The thought of lying to them pulled at the pit in my stomach.

Aunt Jasmine muttered a spell and stepped in front of me, facing my friends.

"We had a break in." Aunt Jasmine said, "but the police have assured us they've already taken the person responsible for this into custody and they'll punish them to the fullest extent of the law."

Sam and Melissa nodded. It was hard to argue with Aunt Jasmine when she sounded so confident. Especially when the enchantment she used to make them believe her words took hold.

"Do you need any help with cleaning up?" Sam asked, dropping the subject of who broke in. I sensed he was more interested in spending time with me and making sure I was alright than cleaning up my demolished house.

"No, but thank you for the offer," Aunt Jasmine said. "Now you two better get home before it gets dark."

Sam and Melissa's eyes both glassed over from the spell Aunt Jasmine used. They nodded and left without another word. Aunt Jasmine groaned as she looked at the devastation. I sighed as well, but for a different reason.

I understood the need for secrecy, but lying to my friends like that still made me feel like crap. It felt like they didn't—couldn't—know the real me.

We cleaned up the couch stuffing in the living room and picked up pages of torn books. Aunt Jasmine and I made piles of things that were salvageable and things that weren't. I whined when I found my favorite statuette of Hecate in pieces on the floor. We cleaned for an hour and felt like we hadn't made a dent, although the pile of destroyed belongings grew higher.

"This would go a lot easier if we were to say... use magic." I said under my breath.

There was no way I was cleaning the entire house by hand. Especially if I had to keep cutting myself on tiny shards of glass.

Aunt Jasmine turned to me and widened her eyes like she couldn't believe I was suggesting such a thing after I had gotten punished for using magic earlier. To be fair, I didn't know she had heard me. Then she looked around, and her shoulders slumped. My lips turned up into a smirk as I straightened my shoulders back and held my arm up with my palm facing away from me. Aunt Jasmine stopped me before I could utter a word.

"You will not be using magic," she said.

Aunt Jasmine gave me her imposter mom look for the second time this week as I cried in protest, but I begrudgingly stepped out of the way so she could perform the spell. I was too tired to argue any more than that. Aunt Jasmine closed her eyes and exhaled through her mouth slowly.

"*Restituo.*"

Wind whirled around the room. Books reassembled themselves, the statuette pieced itself back together, and every piece of furniture that was destroyed mended itself into perfect condition. The front door even lifted into the air and put itself back on its hinges. When the air calmed the house was back to the way we left it this morning. She sat on the couch that was now in one piece and gave a satisfied sigh. I slumped on the cushion next to her, crossing my arms. Aunt Jasmine put her arm around my shoulders and pulled me close.

"I know what will make you feel better." She gave me a squeeze and went to the kitchen.

I heard her rifle through the cupboard until she made a satisfied sound. She came back to the living room with something behind her back. She held out a box of microwave popcorn for me to admire. A grin came to my lips. Movie night was always a good way to cheer me up, and Aunt Jasmine knew it. We turned on an old black-and-white film, but as much as I tried to concentrate on what was happening, my mind kept going over the events of the day. What was the intruder looking for, and did they find it?

CHAPTER THREE

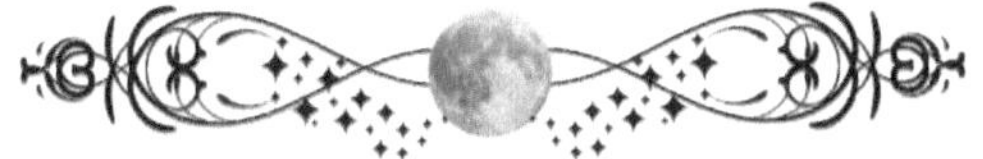

A UNT JASMINE TOOK NOTICE of my appearance the second I walked into the kitchen the next morning and handed me the largest thermos she could find. I filled it with dark roast coffee, cursing the fact there wasn't an Out of Thyme Apothecary anywhere. They made the best energy potions, and right now, I needed their strongest one. My backpack felt like a ton of bricks as I grabbed it off the ground of the entryway and headed sluggishly out of the house.

Sam caught up with me on my way to school. We normally didn't walk together because he liked to be at school early, but I guessed yesterday's scene of furniture debris and glass shrapnel had him concerned. We walked almost a mile with only the leaves blowing and our backpacks bouncing to break the silence. Sam stopped, and it took me a minute to notice. I turned back toward him, a questioning look in my eyes. Sam shuffled his feet and he wouldn't stop running his hand through his hair.

"How long have we known each other?"

"About two months." I said, taking a sip of coffee. Where was this going?

"Right. Well…" He continued to shuffle around. I was not awake enough to play Twenty Questions.

"Spill it weirdo." I said with more force than I meant to.

"I think you're lying to me and Melissa about what happened yesterday."

My body froze up. "Why would I lie about something like that?"

"When your aunt said the police had the guy in custody, I asked my friend's dad—who's a cop—if the force had arrested anyone for breaking and entering lately, and he said no, so it got me thinking," Sam's eyes shifted to mine, and he was no longer nervous. "What else have you been lying about?"

My breathing stopped. I didn't know how to respond. It's not like I wanted to lie all the time, but it was necessary. No one could know what I was. It would put my family, not to mention my entire realm, at risk if humans knew.

I looked into Sam's eyes. I watched the way his hair blew in the cool autumn breeze. He didn't deserve the lies. All he had ever been was nice and welcoming to me.

It had been my third day in this hellhole of a realm and this kid— Sam, he said his name was— would not stop acting like we were best friends. My hand twitched. I wanted to make him bald, or something equally hilarious, but I knew the rules. My uncle, the king of the realm, gave me explicit orders not to use magic of any kind lest the punishment be swift and horrible. So I did nothing to the boy. I sneered in his direction and told him to go die in a hole, though. It didn't bother him one bit. I ground my teeth when he started showing me where my classes were, and every day he came up to me, said hello, and walked me to class. And every day, he got a little less annoying.

As I relived that memory, I realized I wanted his trust more than anything. And it burned a hole in my chest that I could never have it. For the sake of my people, I had to keep what I was a secret. No matter the cost.

"I haven't been lying about anything," I said in an offended tone.

Sam huffed, and his shoulders slumped. "Fine."

He definitely knew something was up. A thought came to mind. Maybe I could get around lying to him and still protect my secret.

"What do you want me to say, Sam?" My tone was sharp, bordering on cruel. "That someone broke through a magical barrier in our house to go looking for some ancient artifact or something? I think you've been reading too many comic books."

Sam's face darkened. That told me everything I needed to know. I wounded him. The look he gave me formed a black pit in my stomach. I wanted to take every word back. I wanted to tell him he was right and that I had been lying, but I knew I never could. The pit went bottomless.

He shoved past me toward school, and I swore I could see tears shimmering in his eyes.

School was the last place I wanted to be, however, so I turned the other way and headed for the one place that felt like home.

I went around the back of the local library and slid in through one of the unlocked windows. It was a school day, so I didn't want anyone to catch me here.

I went to the far back of the building, where Aunt Jasmine sealed it off for construction. At least, that's what she enchanted the staff to believe. In reality, it was where she kept her secret stash. Spell books, history of Amethystia, anything that the human populace shouldn't know about.

With a thud, my backpack dropped to the floor, and I picked up *Your Ultimate Travel Guide to Amethystia: What to Expect and What to Avoid* from one of the shelves. I sat down on the ground, leaning against the bookshelf.

The book had many photos of popular places all across the realm. From the swirling sands of Crowswall Beach to the ethereal plains of Rastanas Valley. I looked at each photo longer than necessary. A single tear escaped down my cheek.

They didn't want me there anymore, so why was I sad?

I turned the page and under the heading "The Royal Family: What You Need to Know" there was a picture of me and my family, minus Aunt Jasmine, She had already moved here. I looked at the portrait and the tears flowed harder. My mom and dad, both of their arms around me, and behind them—looking as regal as ever—my uncle. We looked like a stern, yet happy family. That couldn't have been further from the truth. Mom and Dad always fought about how to handle me. I would get into so much trouble that my old school wanted to expel me for using too much magic. And that was hard to do in a school full of magic users.

My uncle was the only one I had ever looked up to. Even when I got into trouble for creating a golem that smashed through half of the palace, he had given me a lecture with a gleam in his eyes that said, "You did good." I never felt like I wasn't enough around him.

I slammed the book closed and wiped my eyes with shaking hands. My parents and I were never a family. A family wouldn't just shove their daughter off to some distant, foreign land. They wouldn't just abandon her without ever calling and checking in. I didn't have parents anymore. The shaking turned to sobbing as I curled my knees up to my chest and let the tears flow.

I was in this position crying for what felt like forever when I heard a noise a couple of aisles down. My head snapped up. I tried to calm myself the best I could. No one should be back here. No one *could* get back here with the protection charms in place. I stood and wiped the tears away. Whoever was back here would not see me cry, but I would see them in tears after I was done with them. I grabbed my twenty-pound backpack and crept toward the sound.

Someone was reading a book in the middle of the aisle. It was darker back here than in the rest of the library, but the figure stood tall and broad. He was definitely a man. My muscles tensed and my breathing stopped. I was sure he was the one who trashed the house. My backpack was in the perfect position to heave it at the man's head when I saw a streak of white cutting against long, dark brown hair. Only one person I knew of had that trademark. The backpack slid out of my hand with a thud and my uncle snapped the book shut and turned toward me with lightning speed.

"Ebony?" he asked in his deep timbre. "Why aren't you in school?"

I didn't answer because I was too busy throwing myself into his arms. For the first time since I've been in the human realm, the tears running down my face were from joy. He chuckled and wrapped his arms around me.

"I'm guessing this world has been a little difficult for you."

"Not at all," I said through a snotty nose.

"Well," he said, breaking the embrace and looking me in the eye with the gleam I knew so well, "I guess you wouldn't be ready to come home then?"

My face must have shown how happy I was, because he chuckled. "'Not at all', huh?"

My face plummeted. He was baiting me and I fell for it. He lifted my chin so he could look me in the eye. My eyes focused everywhere but on his face.

"My little Earthquake. Look at me."

His nickname for me had me doing as I was told. I noticed the similarity between us. Our eyes were both light, but his were more gray while mine were more blue. Both had the spark of a rebel who could easily cause mayhem. His skin was tan, a trait he got from my dad's, his brothers, side of the family while I got my olive coloring from my mom.

"You will come home," he said, "after your punishment ends. But first, I need your help."

The gleam in his eye vanished and I understood the change in his tone. He wasn't talking to me like my uncle anymore. He was talking to me as king of Amethystia. I matched his tone and nodded once.

"Good," he said. "Now let's go find your she-devil of an aunt before I explain any more."

We found her shelving books in the New Age section. Aunt Jasmine was taking a book from the top of a very large stack. She didn't notice us standing there, so I called her name. She looked over in surprise, and her face registered even more shock when she saw Uncle Hesperus standing next to me.

She put the book she was shelving back on the cart and walked over to us, pointedly staring at me. She was trying to ignore Uncle Hesperus altogether.

"Ebony, what are you doing here? It's a school day."

"I pulled her out early," Uncle Hesperus said. He gave me a side wink. I gave him a weak smile in return.

Aunt Jasmine checked her watch and pursed her lips. "Very early. It's only eleven am."

"I needed her help. I need yours too."

Aunt Jasmine licked her lips and swallowed hard. "I'm afraid that won't be possible."

I knew she was trying to be polite. Even though she had left Amethystia, Uncle Hesperus was still her king. She still had to show him respect. I didn't know what went down between them, but I knew it had something to do with Aunt Jasmine leaving.

"And I'm afraid you have no choice," Uncle Hesperus said in a commanding tone.

Aunt Jasmine clenched her jaw and opened and closed her fists several times before speaking.

"Fine. Let's talk."

She led us to the back where Uncle Hesperus and I had just been. We sat around one of the tables, and Aunt Jasmine looked at Uncle Hesperus impatiently, waiting for him to begin.

"There's been some unrest back home." he started. His face was grave and his eyes had a faraway look, like he was somewhere else entirely.

"People have been whispering about some witch hunters from the human realm having a way to reach us. Those rumors have sparked some... distrust toward the leadership—"

"You mean distrust toward you." Aunt Jasmine said.

"I mean distrust toward us all. Especially the two members of the royal family who have constant contact with humans."

My back straightened. "They suspect us?"

Uncle Hesperus nodded.

Aunt Jasmine scoffed. "I'm not surprised. They haven't liked our family ever since you came into power."

"We need to stop blaming each other. Our family needs to unite, now more than ever."

"How are we supposed to be united when you sent your own niece into exile?" Aunt Jasmine spat.

I flinched. I knew my punishment was only temporary, but that didn't stop me from thinking it wasn't. Aunt Jasmine must have seen. She sat back in her chair and took a deep, calming breath, and smiled at me apologetically.

I nodded with a slight curve to my lips, silently telling her I knew she didn't mean it, but she was right. How were we supposed to quell the fears of the realm when we couldn't even come together as a family?

"I did what I had to. Not what I wanted to. A lesson that you still haven't learned," he said, his deep voice booming.

"You're right. I never learned that lesson. I'm not an Amberwood. Not by blood or marriage. I changed my name because my sister asked me to when she married your brother." Aunt Jasmine's voice was getting louder with every word. Even with the enchantments, people would soon take notice.

"Okay, enough!" I pounded the table. "I don't care if you two hate each other, but right now, we have bigger things to worry about."

"Ebony is right." Uncle Hesperus said. "We need to find those witch hunters and we need to stop them."

"How?" I asked.

"I have two suspects in my sights right now. They go to your school. Sam Freeman and Melissa McFadden."

CHAPTER FOUR

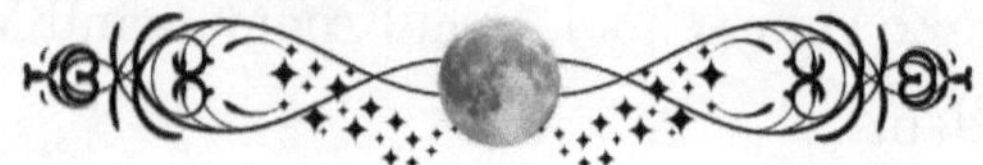

SAM AND MELISSA WERE witch hunters? No way. They were my friends. I've known them both for months. They seemed so boring. So *normal.* Like, more normal than humans had a right to be.

The more I thought about it, the more it made sense, though. Of course, they needed to seem normal. They didn't want to draw attention to themselves. They had to be friends with me. What was that saying about keeping your enemies close?

Maybe they had a hidden room full of weapons to hunt witches down. Maybe they were going to use them on me one day when I was sleeping over. By the time I had gotten over my shock at who the witch hunters possibly were, another thought popped into my head. Why? What did we do to them? What did I do to them?

I spaced out as Uncle Hesperus and Aunt Jasmine talked. Well, *talked* seemed like an understatement. They were full on arguing. Aunt Jasmine didn't want to get involved, and she didn't want me involved either. However, if Melissa and Sam were witch hunters, then this already involved me. Uncle Hesperus kept trying to convince her he couldn't stop them alone.

I yelled to get their attention. Even though we were in a library and yelling should have gotten us kicked out, the charm Aunt Jasmine put in place was amazing at changing the humans perception. But only to a point, so I quieted my voice immediately.

"Would anyone like to know what I have to say?" I asked, a sharp undertone in my voice.

They had the decency to look embarrassed. Good.

"Yes, of course. Go ahead, Ebony," Uncle Hesperus said.

I took a deep breath. "I want to help. If someone is threatening my family, no matter who it is, then they need to be brought down."

I still didn't like it, and neither would Sam and Melissa if they ever found out we suspected them. Which they wouldn't. What was one more lie in the vast ocean of lies I had already told them?

"What about Sam and Melissa?" Aunt Jasmine asked, as if reading my thoughts.

"What about them?" I tried to say as nonchalantly as possible.

"They're your friends. You would really risk that friendship over something that your *uncle* said."

"I take offense to that," Uncle Hesperus said.

"You should."

"Guys! Enough! If they are witch hunters, then they're not friends. They're enemies. I want to do this. Now what's the plan?" I asked Uncle Hesperus.

He took two glowing bugs out of his pocket. They looked like ladybugs except they were shifting purple and blue tones.

"These are Seers Larvae," Uncle Hesperus explained. "Simply put them in your friends' houses and we will see and hear everything that goes on."

"That's illegal," Aunt Jasmine said.

"That's cool," I said at the same time.

He dropped the bugs into my hands. "Have your friends invite you over. Then just drop one bug on the floor in each house, and we'll be good to go."

I nodded as I closed my hand around the bugs. I would do this. There was no choice. I would see my people safe. Even if it meant I lost people I cared for.

Aunt Jasmine told me to go to school, since it was lunchtime. She said she would call and make an excuse about why I was out. I should have known she wouldn't buy Uncle Hesperus's explanation. I asked what Uncle Hesperus would do the rest of the day. His answer wasn't very clear, so I shrugged it off and headed to class.

I swerved through the crowded halls to my locker, grateful that no teachers came up to and asked me why I was tardy. I was trying to think of a plan

41

where I could get Melissa and Sam to ask me over. It didn't think it would be that hard. Melissa and I hang out at each other's houses all the time and Sam tutors me. Sam. I had almost forgotten about our argument this morning. Would he hate me if he knew what I was doing? What was I thinking? Of course, he would hate me. They both would. Unless they already did, and in that case, it was a moot point.

I bounced back into reality just in time to run into a boy, spilling his stuff onto the ground with a loud thud.

"Watch it!" I spat.

"I'm sorry, but I believe it was you who bumped into me," the boy said.

My heart skipped a couple of beats. I was looking at the hottest guy ever. He had messy blonde hair, although it looked like he styled it that way, and deep brown eyes, like dark chocolate, set in a broad, friendly face. He had an accent, though I couldn't place it. It sounded almost British, which made him even hotter. I tried to go around him, but he blocked my path.

"You're the new girl, Ebony, right?"

"What about it?" I asked.

"I'm new too. My name is Fabian. Fabian Proctor. And I just have to say you are one stunning creature."

"Thanks," I said, once again trying to get around him. Once again, he blocked my path. I pursed my lips. This boy needed to get out of my way before something happened to him.

"Need something?"

"Your number." He looked me up and down, checking me out.

"Weak line, Romeo. I'm not interested. Now get out of my way. I'm going to be late for class."

He moved to the side, and I brushed past him as fast as I could so he wouldn't see a smile come to my lips.

As I made my way through the day, I couldn't stop the fluttering in my stomach whenever I thought about Fabian. It was like he had gotten into my head and was a permanent fixture there. I didn't want to admit I liked it.

The last bell rang, and I nearly sprinted to get my stuff. I had forgotten about the Seers' Larvae, and I had to catch Melissa before she left. I didn't have to worry though, because she was waiting for me at my locker.

"Hey," I said, my breathing labored.

"I know your secret," she said in a singsong voice.

I stopped dead. Which secret? Did she know I was lying about the break-in or was she aware that I was going to spy on her, or was she talking about *the* secret? Was she going to blow her cover as a witch hunter?

"Everyone's talking about your encounter with Fabian Proctor," she continued, and I let out a small sigh. I wouldn't call us flirting a secret, but if it occupied her mind, I'd go with it.

"There's nothing to talk about. He's a jerk," I said.

"A hot jerk. I mean, have you seen his jawline? I could cut paper with that jawline."

I rolled my eyes and tried to hide my smile. "Okay. So maybe he is a little cute."

"You're sleeping over at my house tonight, and you're going to spill everything." Melissa slung her arm over my shoulders and squeezed tight.

And just like that, the plan was in motion. I just hoped this was going to be a normal sleepover and not a torture session (either literally or figuratively), but my family needed me to do this.

I went home and got some clothes together. Uncle Hesperus reminded me once again how to use the larvae, and I was off to a sleepover with my enemy.

Melissa and I were in her bedroom, and she was scrutinizing me. I asked her what the problem was, and she just shrugged.

"Okay, what is it?" I asked after another five minutes of her staring at me.

"Nothing," she said. "You just look, I don't know, different. Like there's a sparkle in your eyes that wasn't there before."

"A sparkle? Have you been reading those vampire stories again?"

"Maybe, but you're deflecting. I know who put the light in your eyes, and his name is Fabian." She threw a handful of pretzels in her mouth.

"He ran into me and then he wouldn't let me get around him." I said, grabbing a drink from her mini fridge.

"Is that all?" she asked.

I popped open the soda and took a long sip. "Well, he gave me this corny line about wanting my number."

Melissa squealed, and I couldn't help but smile. The rest of the night we talked about how shiny his hair was, and how perfectly dressed he was in his designer clothes. After an hour and a half of us discussing boys, Melissa's dad came in and told us it was time for bed. Melissa went to the bathroom to brush her teeth, so I had the perfect moment to place the bug without her noticing.

All I had to do was drop it on the floor. That was it. So why couldn't I do it? Why couldn't I just reach into my pocket and pull it out? Why did I have this horrible pit in my stomach? My family needed me to do this. I had to do this to find out if she and Sam were planning something, and what it was if they were. My muscles were tensed and ready, but I wasn't moving.

My shoulders slumped forward in defeat. I couldn't do it. More than that. I didn't want to betray their trust. I'd lie to them because I had to, but I wouldn't spy on them. That was an invasion of privacy even I couldn't stomach. Melissa came back into the room at that moment and I tried to smile as best I could. She noticed my grimace and asked if I was feeling okay. I nodded and slid into bed. All I needed was a good night's sleep.

The next morning, I awoke happy. I'd never had that much fun before. Just talking about boys and laughing so hard your stomach hurt. It felt nice. And then I remembered what I had to do. What I didn't do. And I felt the knot form in my stomach again.

Melissa and I got to school, and Sam was already there waiting. I wanted to apologize to him, but I wanted to do it when we were alone. Melissa asked how he was feeling and if he should even be at school because apparently he got sick and went home early yesterday. He said it was something he ate, and he was feeling much better. I wish I was. The knot grew tighter as the school day progressed. I felt like I was going to throw up when the last bell rang.

My feet dragged me home, delaying the inevitable. I stopped on the sidewalk outside of the house and squared my shoulders. I had to tell Uncle Hesperus that I couldn't do what he wanted me to. After taking a deep breath, I entered the house.

I stopped short when I saw someone sitting on our couch.

Well, some*one* wasn't the right term. He was a Regelf, a race of half elf, half witch hybrids, often looked down upon by witches and elves alike. This Regelf had deep tan skin, like he had spent hours upon hours in the sun. Which made sense with his muscular body. He looked about my age, maybe a year older, with a boyish charm. His pointed ears poked through his long, lavender hair, and his eyes were almost the same shade. I called out for Aunt Jasmine, but I got no answer. Uncle Hesperus, however, came out of the kitchen with a smile.

"Ah, Ebony! Just in time. Let me introduce you to Nightshade Oakenheart. He will be your bodyguard from now on." The Regelf stood and gave me a formal bow.

I stood there, stunned. "Bodyguard?"

"Yes, with the bugs in place, I needed to know you were safe if the day came that the humans found them."

I laughed once without humor. "About that. I didn't do it."

"Didn't do what?" Uncle Hesperus asked, a frown forming on his face.

"I didn't—couldn't plant the bugs." I took a deep breath. "Their trust means far too much to me. I won't betray that. We'll find out for sure if they're the witch hunters we're looking for, but we'll do it another way."

Uncle Hesperus looked troubled. "You already are, though, aren't you? By lying to them about what you are, you're betraying their trust right now. Did you forget they're also trying to kill us? Trying to kill you?"

I knew he was right, but I didn't want to hear it.

"I won't do it." I turned and slammed the door as I left the house.

I was halfway to the library when I decided that was not where I wanted to go. Aunt Jasmine still had my cell phone, so with a huff, I turned around and willed my feet to walk the three miles to Sam's house. He and Melissa needed to know the truth.

The pale yellow house was small but quaint. My hands were shaking. I was so stupid. What was I thinking? If Uncle Hesperus hadn't exiled me permanently before, he would when this was over.

I knocked on the door with a shaking hand, and Sam's mom appeared. She smiled warmly and told me to come in. Sam was sitting at the kitchen table doing his homework. He looked up, surprised when his mom said I was here. She left us alone. I stood there, shuffling my feet and fidgeting until Sam gestured for me to sit down.

"What's up?" he asked after a minute.

"I need to talk to you. Apologize. But I need you to call Melissa over here first," I said.

"Melissa? Why?"

"Please. I'll explain when she's here."

Ten minutes later, and Melissa walked up the concrete path to the front door. She looked as confused as Sam did. I told them we needed a place where we could be alone. Somewhere with wide open space. Sam and Melissa looked at each other. They knew the perfect place.

The grove was about a five-minute trek from Sam's backyard. Melissa tried talking to me on the way there, but I couldn't form words. My heart felt like it was leaping out of my chest and my lips trembled.

We made it to the grove, and they stared at me, curious but impatient. I had to take several deep breaths before I could speak.

This was it. "I know you guys know that I'm keeping something from you. And you're right." I looked at Sam hoping I came across as earnest. His brow was scrunched in confusion. "I'm so sorry. When you said that I was lying, I wanted to tell you the truth, but I couldn't."

"Ebony, what are you talking about?" Melissa asked.

My hands shook at my side. I could do this.

"I'm not what you think I am."

"Yes, you are," Sam chimed in. "You're Ebony. You're a badass and, when you want to be, the kindest, most caring person on the planet."

Tears welled up in my eyes. I didn't know that was how he saw me. It made this even harder because he wouldn't see me like that in a minute.

"I'm a witch," I said, my voice catching.

"So you can be a witch. What girl can't?" Sam said. Melissa shot him a dirty look.

I shook my head. Tears were flowing now. "You don't understand. I'm a literal witch. I was born in a different realm, and I can do magic. My uncle sent me here because I broke a rule I shouldn't have, and I'm doing it again right now. I'll be lucky if my uncle doesn't execute me for this because he thinks you want to kill us, but I don't want to lie to you guys anymore. You're my best friends and I've never had that before. I didn't know what to do because you both have been so nice and trusting and I've just been deceiving you." I couldn't see either of their faces because I was crying so much.

"Yeah right." Sam said. He didn't say it in a mean tone, but it was obvious he didn't believe me.

"I think—" Melissa said, stepping forward, "I think she's telling the truth, Sam."

Sam stalked past Melissa and didn't stop until we were a foot apart.

"Prove it," he said.

I took a steadying breath. Of course, it wouldn't have been as easy as telling them. At least they hadn't laughed in my face or just completely blown me off. They were willing to listen.

I stepped back from Sam and shooed them back with my hands. Once they were far enough away, I calmed myself the best I could. Emotions controlled magic, and I didn't want to hurt them by not being in control of mine.

I held my arms out to either side, palms up.

"*Electricitas!*"

Electric currents shot out of my hands in columns toward the sky. The air crackled between the three of us, and Melissa's normally perfectly styled hair went frizzy with static. I clenched my fists quickly, putting the deadly dancing lights out. I lowered my arms back down to my sides and waited for their reaction.

Sam was the first to speak, although he had to swallow first. "Do-do you do that kind of thing often?"

I nodded.

"Wow," was Melissa's only response. I walked back to them, gauging their reaction. They didn't flinch or run. I took that as a good sign. We all sat down in a circle and just absorbed what happened. They tried to process what I was, and I was having a mental breakdown of what I had shown them. I was dead. If Uncle Hesperus didn't kill me, Aunt Jasmine would. Keeping the secret was one thing they could agree on. The silence was deafening. I didn't want to speak first in case that sparked an adverse reaction out of them. Like screaming. Or gathering firewood for the stake.

"So..." Sam started. "You're a witch. With magic. And you can shoot lightning out of your hands." He exhaled. "Okay."

"Okay?" I asked, my eyes bugging out of my head.

"Yeah." Melissa said, putting her hand on my knee. "Okay."

"You guys aren't like... freaking out?"

"Oh, we're freaking out, but you're still Ebony and we still love you," Sam said, a blush painting his cheeks. Melissa didn't notice.

Tears clouded my vision once more. I loved these two. There was no way they were witch hunters.

After a lot of tears, hugs, and laughter, we went back to Sam's house and hung out in his small living room. Even after revealing the fact that I was a witch to them, I knew I was still hiding behind secrets. I needed to tell them about my uncle's plan for me to spy on them. I was working up the courage when someone started pounding on the front door. Sam answered, and a second later, Aunt Jasmine burst into the living room.

She had a black eye, a split lip, and her hair, which was normally in a sleek ponytail, was all over the place. Her clothes were in tatters, and she had cuts all over her body. She had been crying too because her eyes were still wet with tears.

"Oh my god, Aunt Jasmine!" I leaped up and ran to her. "What happened?"

"I was on my way home from work when someone attacked me. I got back to the house and I couldn't find you. Hesperus said you stormed out, and I thought—I thought." She choked back a sob. "I'm glad you're alright, but we have an enormous problem."

"What kind of problem?" I asked warily.

"Is it a wit—" Melissa asked, but I shot her a look to shut up.

"It's a... family problem, I'm afraid." Aunt Jasmine said. "And I need Ebony home immediately."

CHAPTER FIVE

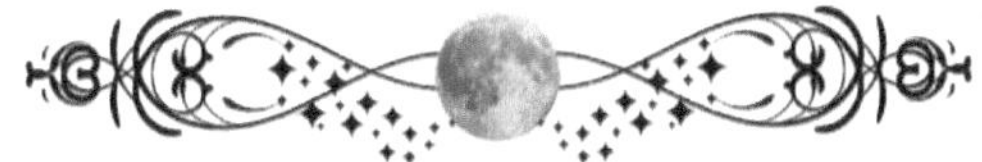

W E GOT BACK TO the house only to find Uncle Hesperus poring over a book, and Night-something-or-other pacing the living room. They both looked up with a sigh of relief when they saw us come in.

"Okay," I said, turning toward Aunt Jasmine. "What happened?"

"A witch hunter attacked me." Aunt Jasmine said. "And it wasn't Sam or Melissa." She looked pointedly at Uncle Hesperus.

Uncle Hesperus nodded, like the revelation that my friends were innocent was no surprise to him. I'd never wanted to slap him so much in my life.

"What did this hunter look like?" the Regelf asked.

"Okay listen up, Nightlight Brokenheart," I said with so much venom in my voice, it surprised me. "We don't need your help. This is a family matter. You can go."

"My name is Nightshade Oakenheart, and your parents assigned me to keep you safe. While I am here, though, I want to protect your family as well."

"Well, marvelous job!" I spat. He was lying. My parents didn't care enough about me to send a bodyguard.

"Enough Ebony!" Uncle Hesperus commanded. I flinched back. "I won't tolerate your attitude right now. This is serious. More serious than I thought."

He said that last part more to himself than to me, but I had never been yelled at by my uncle before. Lectured, yes. But never yelled at. I wanted to shrink inside myself.

"I do not take offense to what she has said." Whatever-shade said. "She is just scared. And it is understandable, given what we are dealing with."

I narrowed my eyes at him. He was right, and I hated it. I opened my mouth to retort, but Aunt Jasmine squeezed my shoulder in warning.

Uncle Hesperus may have been family, but he still commanded us. And he could punish us in ways I didn't even want to imagine, so I held my tongue.

"The witch hunter wasn't anyone I've seen before." Aunt Jasmine said, squaring her shoulders.

"Are you sure?" Uncle Hesperus asked. "This is a small town."

"It's not as small as you think."

Uncle Hesperus slammed his fist down on the kitchen table. I recoiled. I had never seen him this angry.

"My king," Purplehair McPointyears chimed in, "perhaps it would be better if you and your family went back to Amethystia. You all would be much safer there than you are here."

Uncle Hesperus furrowed his brow and stroked his chin. He couldn't seriously be considering Purpleshade Bleedingheart's request, right?

"Maybe you're right." Uncle Hesperus said. "Jasmine, Ebony, pack some stuff, just essentials. We leave in an hour."

"I'm not leaving." Aunt Jasmine lifted her chin in defiance. "This is my home, and no witch hunter is going to run me out of it."

"Same here," I said, crossing my arms. "If it's a fight they want, it's a fight they're going to get."

Uncle Hesperus regarded both of us. He sighed in defeat and muttered something about the women of the family being too stubborn for their own good. He looked at the Regelf and told him to watch out for us. Especially me. A groan escaped my lips. Uncle Hesperus told us he was going back to our realm to update everyone on what was transpiring here. My teeth dug into my bottom lip.

"Don't worry, my little Earthquake." Uncle Hesperus said. "I'll return soon." He turned toward the back door and said, "*Porta Amethystia!*"

The back door swung open, and instead of the deck that led to the backyard, there was a portal. A rainbow of colors, all glowing and swirling around each other, ready to take the caster where he wanted to go.

Uncle Hesperus looked at us over his shoulder. His eyes shifted to me as his long hair swirled around his face. He nodded once. It was his way of saying "stay safe". I nodded back, saying the same. He strode into the portal, which disappeared in a flash of light as soon as he went through.

I woke with a start, but it was still night out. I looked at the clock by my bed. Three thirteen am. Great. I flopped back against my pillow when a rustling caught my attention. I was about to scream when Nightshade spoke.

"It is just me," he said. "I heard some noise and so I came to check on you. What was it that disturbed you?"

Nightshade never used contractions when he spoke. But right now, it almost gave me a sense of calm. I turned back over and sat up, hugging my knees to my chest, and sighed.

"I don't know," I said finally. "I guess the fact that whatever's out there, *who*ever's out there, is going to come back."

"No question." Nightshade agreed. "But when they come back, I will protect you."

"How can you protect me from an unknown enemy?"

"I will make them known." He said it so nonchalantly that I wanted to believe him.

I rolled my eyes. "It's not that simple, dummy. They know we know they're after us now."

"I did not understand any of that." Nightshade said with a chuckle. "But I understand why you are scared. And I can help."

He came to sit at the edge of my bed and held out his hand, palm up. I put my hand in his, and his other hand covered mine. I felt pressure on my palm. He started humming a tune, and I felt instantly calmed.

"I thought only witches could do magic." My voice was barely a whisper.

"Witches can do what other races cannot. It is true. They perfected the craft, and have used it the longest, but regelves are witches too. Besides, this is not magic. My mentor taught me this." He started humming again.

"If it's not magic, then what is it?" I asked after a while.

Nightshade smiled. "I am just using the natural energy that the earth gives out."

"But there's no natural magic in the human realm, right?"

"There is, if you know where to look." Nightshade held my eyes and started humming again. I yawned. He helped me lie down, and I fell asleep, my hand still in his.

I woke the next morning feeling refreshed. I bounded down the stairs and skipped into the kitchen, where Aunt Jasmine was making breakfast.

"You're in a good mood," Aunt Jasmine said.

"I just slept well."

"Good. Oh, before I forget." She placed a device on the counter. My cell phone. "It's been more than a few days, and I think you've proven yourself trustworthy." My stomach fell. She didn't know that I told Sam and Melissa I was a witch yet. So much for trustworthy.

I took it enthusiastically and thanked her. I sat on the couch and turned it on. Fifty-seven new texts and fourteen voicemails. All since yesterday. Oops. I guess seeing Aunt Jasmine in that state worried Sam and Melissa more than I originally thought. I went upstairs where Aunt Jasmine couldn't hear and called Melissa first.

"Thank god!" she said after the first ring. "I thought something had happened!"

"Nothing happened. Well, nothing *more* happened. Aunt Jasmine just forgot to give me back my cell phone until now."

I heard her sigh heavily, and then I heard rustling in the background. Someone groaned.

"Is Sam there with you?" I asked.

"Yeah! He was worried about you too, and we thought maybe you would come back to Sam's, so I slept over."

"Everything's fine," I assured her.

"Good. So, Sam and I decided last night that we were going to go to Presto Espresso for breakfast. Want to join us? Please say yes!"

I laughed. "Of course I'll go with you guys!"

Melissa squealed, and Sam groaned. He wasn't a morning person.

I got dressed and was about to head out when I noticed Nightshade by the door, waiting.

"No." I groaned. "You are not coming with me."

"My job is to protect you. I need to be with you in order to do that job," he said simply.

I complained to Aunt Jasmine, saying it wasn't fair, but she told me he had to escort me. Probably because she didn't want to deal with him herself. I stomped my foot on the ground like a petulant child, but accepted my fate.

Presto Espresso was a tiny hole in the wall. Sam and Melissa had introduced it to me when I had first moved here, and I instantly fell in love with the coffee. The atmosphere, however, was not my style.

It looked like aspiring indie artists used this place to practice their setup, with the exposed brick walls and the fairy lights hanging overhead. Vinyls hung on the wall, all signed by their respective artists, and indie pop played in the background. I tried to ignore it as best I could and found Sam and Melissa in their usual booth in the back.

Nightshade and I slid into the empty seats of the dark green booth, him next to Sam, and me next to Melissa. Sam shifted in his seat, and would look everywhere but at Nightshade.

"So," I started. "This is Nightshade. He's my bodyguard."

"Boyfriend," Nightshade corrected. Huh?

"Bodyguard?" Melissa asked, shocked.

"Boyfriend?" Sam echoed Melissa's shock. Nightshade shot me an alarmed look.

"No." I nudged Nightshade. Hard. "Bodyguard."

"Why does he have pointed ears?" Sam asked in a stage whisper.

"Well, he's a Regelf. They all have pointed ears."

Melissa and Sam's mouths dropped open.

"The magical realm, Amethystia, has many creatures living in it, not just witches." I explained further.

"Wow." Melissa mouthed.

Nightshade was watching this exchange with a troubled look on his face.

"What's up?" I asked him.

"These humans know about you?"

I sunk into the booth, realizing I had forgotten to warn Nightshade about Sam and Melissa. I explained everything that had happened until I told my friends the truth and begged him to not say anything to my aunt or uncle. He didn't look too convinced, but he also said he'd keep it quiet.

We ordered our food and caught up with each other. Sam was tutoring Melissa before school because she was failing biology. I was also failing bio, but Sam didn't need to know that. The last thing I wanted was to get to school earlier than necessary. It turned out Nightshade was pretty cool, too. A bit of a nerd since he told us he graduated top of his class at Progarria Academy—the best school in Amethystia for anyone who wanted to become a part of the royal guard.

Technically, my family was royal and technically I was a princess, but I hated that title and I refused to call my uncle King Hesperus. It sounded so pretentious. However, when Sam and Melissa found out my title, they were practically talking over each other, calling me "Your Highness" and apologizing for not using my title when talking to me. I shut that down real quick. The last thing I wanted was for my friends to feel obligated to me.

I also found out Nightshade had several siblings, and he talked fondly of them. It made me smile.

The way he talked about having siblings seemed so nice.

We had stayed there for over an hour when some weirdo walked into the cafe. They were wearing all black, and I mean *all* black. They had a black long-sleeved shirt, black pants, and a black hood with a mask to cover their face. The only thing not covered in black were their bright green eyes, and when they locked onto me, all the color drained from my face.

"Guys," I said urgently. "Get out of the booth and go out the back. Now."

"Why?" Sam asked, straining over the seat to see. "What's wrong?"

Nightshade saw my face and instantly went on the defensive. He ushered my friends out of the booth quickly, and he and I followed.

The person followed us out the back into the alleyway. Nightshade roughly shoved us all out of the way as the person in black went for an immediate attack. They used a sword I had never seen before. It had weird shapes carved into it. They looked like sigils, but I didn't recognize any of them. Nightshade blocked the attack with his arm. I gasped. I thought for sure that the sword would have lopped his forearm off, but upon closer inspection, he was wearing armor underneath his clothing.

Nightshade did a backflip to get away from the attacker. He held out his arm and a glowing blade made of Dark Stone formed. I had only seen Dark Stone twice. It was rare to find and forging it was damn near impossible. Dark Stone was found in the depths of caves that were littered with the most heinous demons, and even if someone managed to evade those demons and retreive some Dark Stone, only the best blacksmiths could even work with it.

Nightshade swung the blade at our assailant, but they dodged. They parried and locked blades with Nightshade. The sigils on the attacker's sword glowed. Smoke appeared, and the assailant's blade caught fire. The attacker leaped back and stared at the sword. They then swung at Nightshade again, and while the blade didn't touch him, the fire did. Nightshade yelled in pain and grabbed his cheek, dropping his sword and leaving him defenseless. The attacker advanced slowly, knowing they had the advantage.

I watched the scene in horror. Nightshade didn't deserve to die. I didn't want my friends in harm's way, either. I lunged forward, far enough away from Sam and Melissa where no harm would come to them, but far enough away from the attacker so they couldn't see what I was doing. And what I was doing was stupid. Forbidden even. It was the reason I won my duel back home and lost my home altogether.

I held out both hands, palms facing outward. I spaced my feet evenly apart and took a deep breath.

"Hey Emo Wannabe!" The attacker looked over just in time for me to yell, "*Anima magica!*"

The air chilled and the sky darkened. Wind whipped around me like a tornado. My highlighted brown and pink hair blew over my face, but I didn't need to see. I knew where I was aiming. A ball of glowing light formed in front of my palms. It grew bigger and brighter until it was the size of a basketball and as bright as a star. I pulled my arms back over my head and flung them forward, releasing the ball of pure life energy.

It hurled toward our attacker. The assailant's eyes widened, and they were smart enough to run in the opposite direction. They ran toward the end of the alley, but didn't quite make it. My magic caught them in the ribs. They howled in pain, hugged their side, and limped off down the alleyway, slowly enough that we could catch them if we wanted to, but I was so tired. I rested my hands on my knees as my legs trembled. The wind died down, and the sky returned to the normal hue of morning blue. I wobbled over to Nightshade, who stared at me like I was the one who had attacked him.

Sam and Melissa came running up to us with smiles on their faces. Smiles that dissipated when they saw Nightshade's look of fury.

"I did what I had to," I explained.

"A human!" he roared. "They were human, and you used the most powerful magic ever discovered!"

"They were going to kill you!"

"I would have been fine. They will be lucky if they survive the day."

I swallowed hard. I knew he would be angry, but I thought it would have been about me using a forbidden spell, not the life of the person who wanted to kill us.

"What do you mean by that?" Melissa asked.

Nightshade huffed. "Ebony used Soul Sorcery. The king of the realm forbade it a century ago because it is too powerful. And it takes a terrible toll on the caster."

"What kind of toll?" Sam asked.

"Soul Sorcery comes from the life force of the caster, which is why it is so powerful. Ebony just decreased the number of years she will live."

CHAPTER SIX

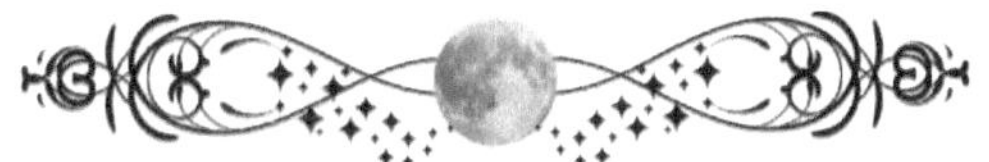

WE ALL SAT AROUND a table in the library, getting a lecture from Aunt Jasmine about how stupid we were, what kind of damage we could have caused, blah blah blah. Well, mostly it was about how stupid *I* was. Sam and Melissa were just caught in the middle of it.

"And Soul Sorcery!" she continued. "I mean really, Ebony, what were you thinking?"

"It was stupid, okay?" I said, just wanting the lecture to be over.

"I couldn't agree more," said a voice behind Aunt Jasmine. We all looked over , but I already knew who it was.

"Uncle Hesperus," I said in a low voice.

He said nothing, but he scowled at me, arms crossed and an eyebrow raised. He set his mouth in a thin line, and I knew he was furious. It was the same way he had looked at me when I had used Soul Sorcery the first time.

I stood in the throne room of the family palace. My parents stood on either side of an intricately carved throne. On the throne sat my uncle, looking like the ruler he was. All three faces had looks of rage and disappointment. Looks that were directed at me.

"Do you have anything to say for yourself?" my father asked.

"I won the duel."

"Is that really what you want to start with?" That voice was my mothers, although it sounded nothing like her usual soft timbre.

Right now, it was loud and harsh. I flinched. My uncle stood and sighed.

"Luna, Horus, let's talk."

My uncle took them off to the side. I didn't hear much, but what I did hear, I didn't like. Words like "exile" and "military camp" were being thrown around. I shuffled my feet while they debated on what to do with me.

After what seemed like an eternity, they stopped whispering and returned to their positions in front of me. Uncle Hesperus didn't take a seat, though. Instead, he took several deep breaths and folded his hands behind his back.

"Ebony Amberwood, you have been found guilty of breaking our realm's most sacred rule and using forbidden magic. Do you have any words before I pass judgment?"

I shook my head. I knew I messed up, but I wasn't sorry. If I had the chance, I'd do it again. My uncle nodded as if he expected as much.

"Then by my decree, as King of Amethystia, I hereby exile you to the human realm—"

"What!" I exclaimed.

"—temporarily," my uncle finished. "You will live with your aunt and maybe she can teach you some of the humanity you obviously seem to lack."

I looked down at my clasped hands. That punishment—this punishment—was bad enough.

I didn't want to think about the retribution my uncle had cooked up for me this time.

"I thought you were back in Amethystia," I said finally, looking up at him.

"I was. Then I felt a witch use Soul Magic in the human realm, and guess how I knew who it was?"

"Telepathy?" I asked, trying to crack a joke. It fell way flat.

"I knew it was you because your aunt wouldn't be that rash. And while we're discussing the subject of foolishness, what are two humans doing here?"

"She told them. Everything," Nightshade said. Traitor.

Uncle Hesperus looked like he wanted to disintegrate me right there. I've never seen him look so angry.

"So not only did you use the most forbidden magic in the realm for a second time, but you told two humans about us?"

I nodded, slowly wishing I could make myself disappear. Uncle Hesperus sat down. I clasped my hands so tightly, my knuckles turned white. I focused on my breathing and the ticking of the clock behind me.

"I don't know what to do with you." Uncle Hesperus said after a minute.

"Love me the way I am?" I suggested.

I looked up at him. He narrowed his eyes.

"No. Since you can't go one day without using magic, I think I'll make you go every day without using magic."

"What does that mean?" I asked.

"I'm taking away your magic. Permanently." Uncle Hesperus said, his face as grim as his voice.

"Hesperus, please think about what you're doing." Aunt Jasmine stepped in. "Magic to a witch... It's like breathing to humans. It's a part of who we are. If you take that away..."

"I know what will happen." Uncle Hesperus replied. "But she needs to learn a lesson, and being exiled obviously hasn't taught her anything."

A cold shock seeped through my body. The only witches ever to have their magic taken away were criminals, and they went insane. He wouldn't do that to me. Would he?

"Please, my king," Nightshade pleaded. "She was only trying to protect me. Why punish her that severely for trying to do the right thing the wrong way?"

Uncle Hesperus looked at Nightshade. More specifically, he was staring at Nightshade's burn. He pursed his lips and inhaled deeply.

"Perhaps you're right. But she isn't going unpunished."

Uncle Hesperus glanced back at me, and his eyes glowed purple. My arm warmed and when I gazed at my skin, a mark appeared. Glowing purple swirls started etching themselves on my wrist, winding their way up my arm in an intricate pattern of whorls and curls. Thorns protruded from the curves, seeping into my flesh. And when it stopped glowing, I gaped at my uncle.

"A Mark of Sealing," he said simply. "I will limit your powers from now on. Nothing but the basics. It will come off when—and if—you've mastered how to control yourself. In the meantime, your aunt will teach you what it means to be a true witch."

"Gee, thanks for asking." Aunt Jasmine rolled her eyes.

"This is so unfair." I crossed my arms in a huff.

"Be grateful I'm not doing much worse, young lady. And as for your friends…"

Sam and Melissa were pale, and they looked horrified. Melissa even looked like she wanted to pee her pants.

Uncle Hesperus sized them up. "I suppose you'll need friends to help you get through this. Besides, they're in danger now, too."

I closed my eyes and let the tension leave my body. I didn't want to get them hurt. Even by my uncle.

"Will you return to Amethystia?" Nightshade asked.

"No. It's obvious there's much that needs my attention here." With that, Uncle Hesperus stood and stormed out of the library.

I swallowed hard. This was not the way I thought today would go. My friends got attacked, my bodyguard got hurt trying to protect me, and I was on magical probation. Tears welled up in my eyes, but I swallowed them down. I would not let my friends see me cry over this. So instead, I stood up and ran out of the library, not knowing where I was going, but anywhere was better than this place.

I ended up at the park, sitting on a bench and watching people jog by. It was midday on a Saturday, so there were families and kids running around on the playground. I found the scene comforting. My phone rang. Once. Twice. Three times. I turned it off.

Someone sat next to me, and I didn't even look to see who it was.

"Not the first place I thought I would find you." Fabian said. My heart skipped a beat. I turned to him. His dark brown eyes gleamed wickedly, and he smirked. His sandy blonde hair blew in the autumn wind, and it made him look straight out of a magazine.

I smirked back. "That's because you don't know me."

"I would like to."

I felt my cheeks go red. He chuckled, and I knew he had noticed.

"I would like that too," was all I said in response.

"Then let's get away from all these people. It's too noisy." He got up and started walking. I thought about what I was doing for a split second, then followed him.

We ended up near a wooded area. The park was still visible, but the voices weren't at all audible.

Fabian faced me and looked me up and down, checking me out. I leaned against a tree, arching my back so my chest would stick out more. He gave me a lopsided smile and put his hands on either side of the tree, trapping me. He leaned closer, and I closed my eyes. Leaning his face into the side of my neck, he trailed his lips along the skin there. I moaned and moved my head to the side in response. He pressed his body closer, squishing me against the tree. He moved his mouth from my neck, trailing his lips along the edge of my jaw. I opened my eyes as he moved his mouth away. His eyes held a hunger, and I bit my lip, challenging him. He smirked and was leaning in to kiss me...

"Can you help me find my mommy?" a little girl asked in tears. Fabian and I stared at her. She was only about seven, and obviously terrified.

I pushed Fabian off of me. He didn't look pleased. Neither was I. I knelt down to the little girl's eye level and told her we would help. Fabian muttered he had somewhere else to be and marched away. I rolled my eyes and held my hand out to the little girl. She put her hand in mine and we walked back toward the playground.

It was easy to spot the girl's mother. She was the only woman in the park shouting and looking around frantically. Their eyes met, and they rushed toward each other. Both mother and daughter were sobbing as they held the other. I thought about how it would have been nice if my parents had cried if I ever got lost as a child.

I walked back to the house. No one was home. I went up to my room and flopped on my bed. Fabian and I were really about to make out. I sighed. Why did that little girl have to interrupt us? I took my phone out of my pocket and turned it on. I had several missed calls, all from Aunt Jasmine. She was worried about where I was. I flung the phone on the nightstand and curled up facing the wall. The mark on my arm made itself known in my peripheral vision. My eyes focused on the dark design. I didn't need it. I knew how to control myself. It was so unfair. I couldn't wait to get home. There were more rules here than back in Amethystia. My phone buzzed with a text, and Melissa's name popped up on the screen.

Melissa: U doing OK?

Me: Yep

Melissa: Good. I want a girls nite. U in?

Me: Omw

I walked up to Melissa's house fifteen minutes later. She answered when I knocked.

"I told your aunt where you would be," she said sullenly.

"Thanks."

We went to her room, and I set my stuff down. It was after five in the afternoon, so we got in pajamas and watched movies in the rec room while we waited for a pizza.

We were watching some romantic comedy when the doorbell rang. Melissa came back with the pizza and we ate and watched the rest of the movie. Well, she ate and watched the rest of the movie. I sat on the brown leather sofa, staring off into space. I didn't know how to handle today's events.

My friends were in danger and I couldn't use magic to help them. I couldn't use magic to save myself.

Melissa noticed my mood, and she wrapped her arms around me. My lips started trembling and my whole body followed. A sob came out of my mouth and tears fell down my face. I hugged her back as the tears came more violently and the sobs got louder. We stayed like that for a good ten minutes until I finally calmed down. She didn't release me. She just kept hugging me, her head resting against mine.

When I could finally tell her I was okay, she let go.

"Are you sure?" she asked, her voice full of concern. I nodded.

"Okay. So, what did you do today?"

I smiled at her, grateful that she wants to take my mind off everything. So I told her where I went and who I ran into and what we almost did.

"No way!"

I nodded, heat rushing to my face.

"How was it?" she asked. "And I want details!"

I told her we got interrupted by a kid and her face fell.

"But he pinned me to a tree."

She squealed again. I enjoyed seeing her happy. I vowed I would never let anything happen to her or Sam.

We went to bed, and awoke the next morning early to make breakfast. Sam knocked on the door around eight. His eyes widened and he took a step back.

"I thought you would have gone home." he said.

"After what happened yesterday?" I asked incredulously. "No freaking way."

Sam nodded. That was the end of that conversation.

It was the start of October, so the three of us went down to Essex Street to check out the festivities there after a healthy breakfast of greasy bacon.

"Oh! There's The Crystal Rune! I want to go in and see all the witchy stuff they have!" Melissa said, heading for the shopfront.

I normally didn't like human magic shops, but The Crystal Rune was pretty cool on the inside. It had herbs of all kinds hanging upside down from the ceiling, drying. The walls were lavender and had a bunch of black and white photos from local artists. My favorite picture was one of the cemetery covered in snow.

Shelves upon shelves around the shop housed crystals of all shapes, sizes, and colors. From jade to rose quartz; they even had bloodstone. Bloodstone was my favorite gem because it promoted courage and resilience. Something I definitely needed after my slimeball of an ex dumped me for a literal banshee.

Melissa was looking at the tarot cards when I walked over to her.

"Only witches can use tarot cards." I whispered. "Why?"

"Because the cards draw from our magic to tell us our paths. That's why each draw is specific to that person."

"So why are there tarot cards here?" she asked.

I shrugged. "Profit. I hate to break it to you, but magic shops in the human realm aren't really magic shops."

"Thanks." She sounded defeated. I told her I would take her to Amethystia and show her a real magic shop sometime. Her face beamed. As

I told her about the potion masters and diviners at the magic shops in Amethystia, Sam wandered over with his arms full of books on the history of witchcraft. When I asked why he had so many books, he shrugged and said he wanted to know more about witches and their history with the town. I rolled my eyes and strolled over to the table housing the pendulums.

We got back to Aunt Jasmine's house after sunset as we didn't want to worry anyone too much, and Aunt Jasmine opened the door before we were even up the front steps. She and I looked at each other awkwardly, then she grabbed me into the biggest hug I've ever gotten. I hugged her back—as much as I could with shopping bags on my arm—and all the tension between us from yesterday fell away.

Aunt Jasmine let Melissa tell her all about the stuff she bought at The Crystal Rune, so while they were talking, Sam and I sat out on the deck. It was a peaceful night; the stars were out in full force, and the October wind was changing from chilly to just cold. I wrapped my jacket tighter around me, and Sam did the same.

It looked like Sam was about to say something, but Melissa came out on the deck and he closed his mouth, staying silent.

The next day, I was on my way to history class—the only class I had with Melissa—and I jumped back at the group of girls standing around the room gossiping, grooming their hair and putting on makeup.

"What's going on?" I asked Melissa as I sat down next to her.

"Apparently, we're supposed to have a new teacher for the rest of the semester, and according to the girls who have seen him, he's supposed to be gorgeous." Melissa said excitedly. My head hit my desk with a thud. I did not want to deal with human girls and their hormones for the next three months.

The bell rang, and I heard the girls slowly make their way to their own classes, just trying to get a glimpse of the new teacher.

"Hello, class."

My head popped up so fast I thought I would throw my neck out. Oh, hell no.

I watched as my uncle wrote an obviously fake name on the board and introduced himself as Mr. Foster. I would have snickered if it hadn't been so appalling. For the rest of the hour, I tried to not blow a gasket but almost failed when he called on me to answer a question.

The bell rang, and I quickly gathered my stuff to leave, thanking Hecate I wouldn't have to deal with him for the rest of the day.

"Miss Amberwood, can I see you for a second?"

I groaned. There went my hasty escape. I walked to his desk, dragging my feet.

"Yes, Mr. Foster?" I asked in an overly sweet tone.

He smiled back. As the last girl left, so did his smile.

"You weren't paying attention today," he said.

"Are you serious? You asked me to hang back because I wasn't paying attention? And by the way, what the hell are you doing here?"

He raised an eyebrow. I knew I was already on thin ice with him, but I couldn't help it. He had no right to invade my school life.

"I'm here because you need to be watched,"

I was about to retort when the door opened. We both whipped our heads to see who was interrupting us. It was Fabian. Heat flooded my cheeks, and I looked down quickly.

Fabian and I hadn't talked since the park, and I didn't want him to bring it up now.

"Hello," my uncle said. "I don't think we've met yet. What can I do for you?"

Fabian smiled and introduced himself. Luckily, all Fabian wanted to know about was his extra credit assignment. Uncle Hesperus gave him a piece of paper and Fabian gave us our privacy once more.

"What happened to Ms. Lewis, anyway?" I asked.

"She decided to... take a vacation," Uncle Hesperus said. I rolled my eyes. Sure she did.

I caught up with Melissa after my talk with my uncle. She wanted to know why he was here. I didn't give her an answer because I wasn't really sure myself. He said he wanted to monitor me, but if that was the case, he could have had Nightshade spy on me.

As soon as I walked in the door, I saw Aunt Jasmine had a bunch of stuff set up. Books on spells and the history of witchcraft, altar settings, and a statuette of Hecate were all set out on the coffee table.

"Hey!" Aunt Jasmine said. She was too cheery. She didn't want to do this any more than I did. I sighed. I wouldn't make this any harder on her, so I sat down on the couch and crossed my legs.

"Hey!" I said back in the same cheery tone. "What's on the agenda today, prof?"

Her face fell. "Don't call me that."

I laughed. Well, maybe I would make it a little hard on her. She handed me a candle carved with the symbol for fire.

"What does fire represent?" Aunt Jasmine asked.

"A hot mess?" I guessed.

Aunt Jasmine raised an eyebrow at me. I squared my shoulders and answered again.

"Fire represents life. Without the sun, there would be no plants, but fire also represents destruction. A single spark can burn down an entire forest."

"Good. And why are there two sides to the same element?"

I slammed the candle down on the table. "What does this have to do with getting this stupid mark off me?"

"You need to learn what it means to be a witch. Witches don't go off half cocked and use Soul Sorcery unless there is an excellent reason to."

"But it was. Nightshade got hurt."

"Nightshade can take care of himself. His job is to protect you, not the other way around."

I sat back and crossed my arms. The argument was going nowhere, and Aunt Jasmine wasn't going to change my mind. I did the right thing.

Aunt Jasmine pursed her lips and went over to the bookshelves. She took down a photo album and flipped the pages until she went, "Ah ha!"

She handed me the book without even looking at me. On the page she flipped to there was a photo of a little girl. Only two. Maybe three. With a huge smile on her face, holding a bright white candle that was almost as tall as her.

"That's you," Aunt Jasmine said when she saw the confused look on my face.

"That can't be me." I slammed the book closed. *The girl in the photo looked happy, for one.*

"It is. You said you wanted to be just like your mom when you grew up so we started training you in magic very early on. Your mom took that photo at your Celestial Ceremony."

"I don't remember that," I said.

The Celestial Ceremony was a huge deal for every witch. It was like a baptism for humans except instead of being dunked in holy water, they dunked young witches in star water, symbolizing the start of their magical journey.

Aunt Jasmine sat down and wrapped me in a hug.

"She was so proud of you, you know."

"Oh yeah, now look at me," I said. "One colossal disappointment."

Aunt Jasmine broke the hug and looked me dead in the eyes. "You are not a disappointment. You're a teenager. A teenager rebelling against society. It's not that big of a surprise."

"You mean, given my parents' *lack* of parenting?" I said icily.

"Given who your family is."

"I wouldn't rebel if you were my mother. Why did you leave?" I asked in a low voice. I had always been curious, but afraid to ask. I wasn't sure I wanted to know the answer.

Aunt Jasmine hesitated and shame flickered across her face. "Because that world wasn't for me," she finally said.

I nodded. She wasn't telling me everything, but I knew she wouldn't tell me anything more, so we moved on.

After what seemed like an eternity of going over the symbolism of the elements and how they affected everyday life for witches, Aunt Jasmine called it quits for the day.

I got into my pj's while Aunt Jasmine made dinner. Nightshade walked through the door as I was coming downstairs. His burn looked a lot better, but it would still leave a scar. He had a worried look on his face.

"What's up?" I asked, stopping at the bottom of the stairs.

"Where is Lady Jasmine?" he asked.

"In the kitchen." He walked away without another word. What was his deal?

I followed him to the kitchen as he put something on the counter. It was a doll. My aunt took one look at it and her face paled. What was so scary about a doll? I went to inspect it. Oh. The doll had a pointed hat on its head and a rope around its neck.

"Who would send that?" I asked.

"Probably whoever attacked you at the café." Aunt Jasmine's voice was soft.

"But... that was weeks ago."

"That was only a few days ago," Nightshade said.

"I thought you said they wouldn't last the day." My voice trembled.

"I said they would be lucky to survive the day. It looks like they were."

"And now they're healed enough to threaten us." Aunt Jasmine threw the doll across the room, and it landed perfectly in the trash can.

I took a deep breath. This wasn't just a threat, it was a promise. They knew where we lived, and they were coming for us.

The days that followed were full of anxiety. Whenever someone walked toward me, I would tense up and get ready for a fight. Then they would pass and I would relax. Melissa and Sam were anxious too. They had received the same dolls outside of their houses. Except theirs didn't have pointed hats.

Richelle was back at school after being out for a week because of a family member dying. She was as mean as ever, which only added to the restlessness.

I filled the time after school with lessons from Aunt Jasmine and hanging out with my friends. We all had decided that it was better if we stuck together as much as possible, given the current atmosphere. Uncle Hesperus spent his nights grading papers and trying to use the dolls to track the witch hunter, but it was no good. They were too smart.

"They have to be using magic," Uncle Hesperus said one day after school.

"They're human. They can't use magic," Aunt Jasmine reminded him.

"Well then, someone else is, because I should have tracked them down by now."

"Or maybe zombies planted it," I said while Sam and I were playing COD Zombies on the PlayStation. Melissa was on the couch going through a fashion magazine.

"Don't you have homework to do?" Uncle Hesperus asked, his voice sharp.

I snickered. "We already did it."

"Yeah. What else is there to do?" Melissa asked.

Uncle Hesperus and Aunt Jasmine had told all three of us it would be better if we didn't go anywhere else but to school and home. So that's what we did. No shopping. No hanging out at the cafe. It was truly hell. Our grades were even going up.

Uncle Hesperus called me into the kitchen. I groaned in protest, but I set the controller down and went to see what he wanted.

"I want you to try using the Seers' Larvae in your friends houses again," Uncle Hesperus whispered.

"What? No! Besides, they've been over here 95% of the time."

"Ebony has a point," Aunt Jasmine chimed in.

"I have no other leads. Please. Just to rule them out?"

I groaned. I knew Uncle Hesperus was getting desperate, and he wanted to go home. Frankly, I did too, and maybe this would help me get there sooner.

"Fine," I conceded. "Just to rule them out."

CHAPTER SEVEN

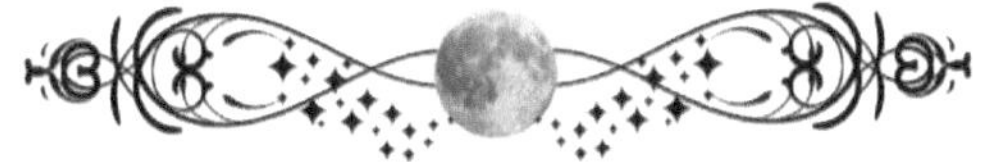

M ELISSA AND SAM HAD gone home hours ago, but Uncle Hesperus wanted the larvae planted tonight, so there I was, trying to sneak in the back window of Sam's house at three in the morning. Nightshade had come along as my lookout and he didn't look thrilled to be there either.

I landed inside the kitchen with a small thud and I followed the hallway into Sam's bedroom. He was sleeping peacefully, his mouth hanging open as he snored softly. I planted the larva on his nightstand. The little blue bug glowed as it came to life. It scurried down the nightstand onto the floor, and I hurried back to Nightshade.

Melissa's house was more difficult. It was two stories, and she slept on the second floor. I had Nightshade plant the bug, because he was more nimble than I was. He used his magic to open the window without a sound, and he slipped in silently. I bounced on my toes, waiting for something to go wrong, but a few minutes later, Nightshade came out of the window just as silently as he went in.

We went back to the house where Uncle Hesperus was still awake and told him it was done. He nodded and his shoulders visibly relaxed. I yawned and went straight to bed with a heavy heart for, once again, betraying my friends' trust.

My eyes snapped open. Realizing I had slept through my alarm, I hurriedly got ready for school and bounded out the door without breakfast.

I caught up with Sam, and my heart gave a little start. Did he know I was spying on him? No, he couldn't know. I was so silent last night, and the bugs were near invisible to humans.

"Hey!" he said in a chipper tone. "You look like you're dead."

"Thanks. Girls love it when boys say that," I said.

He apologized and offered me his coffee. I took it gratefully and gulped it down. Gross. Peppermint.

I handed him the empty cup, and he chuckled. "Didn't get much sleep last night?"

"Just worried about everything going on."

He nodded. As much danger as he and Melissa were in, he knew I was in one hundred times more danger. We walked the rest of the way in silence and split up once we got into the building. The smells of the cafeteria serving a mediocre breakfast of turkey bacon and scrambled eggs wafted into my nose as the sounds of several hundred teenagers chattering filled the air. I went to my locker, and was getting my stuff ready for class when Richelle rammed into me.

"Watch where you're walking, freak," she said, her nose wrinkled in disgust.

"Real original. Get those insults where you got your implants?"

She glared and got so close to my face, I could smell the mint gum coming off her breath.

"What did you say?" she whispered menacingly.

"I'm sorry. Do you need me to text it to you?" I knew I shouldn't have been running my mouth, but she was pissing me off.

"You better watch it," she threatened. "Or we'll see just how long you can hang."

I froze. "What did you say?"

"Now who needs the text? I said if you don't watch it, you can't hang here. Simple." With that lovely threat, she turned and walked away.

I gaped at her retreating figure in confusion. What did she mean by "hang"? Did her threat have anything to do with those dolls? Ugh. I was more exhausted than I thought.

I didn't have time to process her comments because the first bell rang and I hurried off to class.

As I entered history, I was feeling even worse about Richelle's comment. I wanted to show her why she shouldn't mess with me, but the mark burned into my arm reminded me I couldn't. I sat down next to Melissa and slammed my book on the desk.

"What's wrong?"

I didn't want to worry her about Richelle, so instead I said, "I'm just exhausted. Didn't sleep last night."

Melissa nodded and said no more as my uncle brought the class to attention.

Uncle Hesperus was being especially irritating today. Every time he asked a question, he would always call on me to answer. Like I knew what some war in 1812 was called!

After class, he asked me to hang back. We waited until everyone had left the room until we started talking.

"What's with you today?" he asked.

"Me? You're the one who wouldn't stop asking me questions!"

"You weren't paying attention. Again. And you didn't even let any of us know you were leaving this morning."

"Gee, maybe that's because *someone* had me up late spying on the only friends I have! Speaking of... have you found anything yet?"

"Nothing of use." He tapped his fingers on his desk.

"Maybe that's because there's nothing to find," I said. I wrestled with whether to tell him about Richelle's comment to me this morning. Even if it was just a highschool threat, it still bothered me. Just as I was opening my mouth, the warning bell rang.

"Get to class," Uncle Hesperus said. "We'll talk more later."

The rest of the day was a blur. I fought sleep throughout the day, and when the last bell finally rang, I literally dragged my feet to my locker.

Melissa and Sam were there waiting for me. I gave them a half-assed wave.

"Wow." Melissa said. "You look bad."

I nodded.

The three of us walked to my house, with the two of them glancing at me constantly. Probably trying to make sure I would stay upright.

We were about halfway home when we heard a car engine rev. The engine got closer, and we moved to the side to let it pass.

Sam looked behind us and screamed, "Scatter!"

I had just enough time to look behind me and see the car racing toward us.

Melissa dodged to the left, and Sam pushed me down to the right just as the car sped through the area where we had been walking.

My heart thumped. I looked up at Sam, who was lying on top of me and peering down at me with a strange look in his eyes. I wanted to ask him if I had something on my face, but Melissa came up to us screaming, asking if we were okay. Sam promptly got off me with heat in his cheeks.

We got to the house with no further incident. I saw the setup for witch lessons on the table and I plopped down on the couch. All I wanted was sleep.

Uncle Hesperus burst through the front door a few minutes later and scanned the room with wild eyes.

"Are you three okay?" he asked breathlessly.

We all nodded, and he visibly relaxed.

"What do you mean?" asked Aunt Jasmine walking in from the kitchen, drying her hands on a towel.

"They didn't tell you? A car almost hit them!"

Aunt Jasmine looked at us, shocked. She rushed over, dropping the towel on the floor, and pulled me into a tight hug.

"I mean, we didn't die." I tried to pull out of the hug, but Aunt Jasmine held fast.

"How did you know about it?" Sam asked.

"I was on my way here when I saw it," he said. "I tried to track the car down, but with no luck."

Aunt Jasmine let me go and sat down with a huff. "This is getting too dangerous."

"It is my opinion that the three of them would be much safer in Amethystia." Nightshade suggested, coming downstairs.

"Where the hell were you, Mr. Bodyguard?" I bounded up to him.

"I was looking around town. Making sure everything was all right."

"Um, we almost got hit by a car," Melissa said. "We are definitely not alright."

"Taking them to Amethystia is out of the question," Uncle Hesperus said. "I'm not weaving more distrust there by having two humans in my realm."

"Thanks." Sam crossed his arms and set his mouth in a thin line. "These humans wouldn't be in danger if not for you witches."

I felt a pang in my chest. They blamed me. Of course they did. I'm the one who told them about magic, effectively putting them in harm's way. Sam saw my expression and tried to backtrack.

"What I meant was, Melissa and I wouldn't be here if it wasn't for you, Ebony."

Melissa shot him an incredulous look. I rolled my eyes.

"I meant wouldn't be here as in we wouldn't literally be here right now. Like we would be dead."

Melissa finally told Sam to shut up. He did.

I heaved myself off the couch and went over to the altar with the elemental candles and dusty history books on it.

"Are we going to do this or what?" I asked Aunt Jasmine, picking up a piece of raw rose quartz and squeezing it in my hand.

"Are you sure you want to today?" she asked.

"I'm sure I need my magic back."

With that, we started the lesson.

Today, it was all about potions and what a witch could and could not do with them. What herb to use for what potion, and what not to mix.

I knew that mixing aconite and althea root calmed an angry vampire, and I also knew that azalea and bat's head root made a potent love potion, and that Uncle Hesperus banned the use of all love potions after an unfortunate incident with a troll.

I was reciting back to her all the ingredients in an herbicide potion while watching Sam and Melissa do their schoolwork on the table wistfully. It was a sad day when I wished I was doing homework.

We finished up with the lesson right around dinnertime. Uncle Hesperus had been cooking his famous chicken and chives chowder while we were all studying, and it smelled delicious. I was trying to keep my eyes open while we ate, and I think at one point, Sam moved my food so my head wouldn't fall into it.

I hadn't noticed I had fallen asleep, but I felt a pair of arms carry me up to my room. I wanted to open my eyes and protest, but I was so tired that I nestled into the warmth of their chest. The smell of vanilla and musk—a heady combination—filled my nostrils. They laid me down on my bed and put a blanket over me. A smooth, deep voice said something, but I couldn't make out any words.

It was still dark when I woke, and I looked at the clock on my bedside table. It was just before five am. With a groan, I got out of bed and went downstairs, only to find Aunt Jasmine painting in the living room.

"You're up early," I noted.

"I was just about to say that to you." She motioned me over and told me to look at the painting and tell her what I see. I told her all I saw were squiggles in different colors.

"Yes, but what do you *see*? What does the piece make you feel?" she asked again.

I took a better look at the painting. The colors melded together, and I felt warm. Like I was looking at a happy family event.

She smiled when I told her and looked back at the painting, her eyes glowing.

Sam shuffled into the room while we were discussing the appeal of abstract versus realism, and I jumped when I saw him.

"We both stayed the night," Sam said.

I nodded. Of course, Aunt Jasmine and Uncle Hesperus wouldn't want the two of them going home with a crazy person on the loose, especially one who wants to kill them. I lazily wondered what their parents thought about my friends spending the night all the time while Sam and I made breakfast for everyone.

Our kitchen wasn't all that big, so we bumped into each other quite a lot. Sam and I locked eyes while I was putting the bacon on the table, and he had that same strange look on his face that he had yesterday. I shrugged it off and went to tell everyone that breakfast was ready.

School was better today. I wasn't as grumpy, and there were no other thinly veiled threats from Richelle. I even answered a question correctly in history, and Uncle Hesperus seemed pleased.

I got home in a good mood. Melissa and Sam went to go do their homework, and I went to study with Aunt Jasmine.

The start of the lesson went great. We were still working on potions, but as it went on, I got woozy. By the end of the lesson, I wanted to pass out.

"What's wrong?" Aunt Jasmine asked.

I couldn't speak. All I could do was shake my head. I sat down carefully as Sam went to get me some water. I sipped it slowly, unsure if I was going to keep it down. My head pounded. Aunt Jasmine told me I was having a migraine and I just needed to rest. I agreed.

Nightshade took Sam and Melissa home early and was going to watch them for the rest of the night. Aunt Jasmine helped me to bed and then went downstairs to make me a light dinner. Lights were flashing in my eyes, and I held my hands to the sides of my head, hoping my brain didn't fall out.

Uncle Hesperus came home and checked on me. A frown darkened his face, and he fidgeted with his hands while he asked me how I felt. I nodded encouragingly because I was afraid if I opened my mouth, I would vomit.

Aunt Jasmine returned and shooed my uncle from the room. He narrowed his eyes, but left us alone.

I took the cup of soup from Aunt Jasmine's hands and tried to take a sip. I couldn't see behind the lights dancing across my vision, so the soup ended up all over the floor.

Aunt Jasmine cooed and shushed me, trying to make it better, but tears streamed down my cheeks. My head felt like a bowling ball. Noises that were a mix between sobs and groans escaped my lips. Uncle Hesperus came back upstairs and laid his hand on my head. He whispered some words, and the pain slowly subsided. My breathing slowed as my muscled relaxed and my head rested against the pillow. I was getting sleepy. The spots of light dimmed as I slipped into unconsciousness.

Blood filled the rivers, and the sky glowed red from the full moon overhead. The trees had lost their magical glow. Humans and witches alike lay on the cobblestones, dead. Creatures howled from above, and a shadowed figure cackled amongst them. I ran through the blood-soaked streets, slipping on the sticky red liquid. I panted as I tried to reach the Palace, the one place I knew was safe.

The shadowed figure stepped in front of me, blocking my path. He held a sword made of black crystal that was so shiny it reflected the red of the moon perfectly. He rushed toward me. I dodged as quickly as I could, but my leaden feet wouldn't move fast enough. The shadowed figure sliced the blade across my cheek, leaving a warm trail behind.

"Ebony!" I turned toward the sound of my name. Melissa and Sam stood behind me.

"Ebony, run!" Melissa called again.

The shadowed figure rushed for them, quick as lightning. I tried to get to them first, but the more I tried, the slower I became.

I woke up screaming. Aunt Jasmine ran into my room with Uncle Hesperus not far behind. She wielded a baseball bat while his hands were ready to cast magic. They asked me what was wrong, but words didn't come. Sobs escaped my chest, and I hugged my knees, rocking back and forth. They shared a distressed look, and Aunt Jasmine sat by my side, brushing my hair back and telling me everything was going to be okay. I shook my head. Nothing was going to be okay. I felt it in the pit of my stomach. Something bad was going to happen, and I was pretty sure I only caught a small glimpse of what was going to take place.

CHAPTER EIGHT

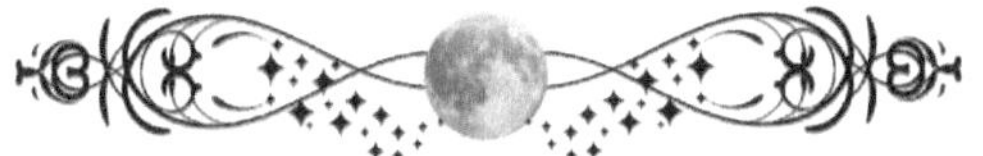

MY AUNT AND UNCLE agreed to keep me out of school for the next few days. During the day, I would be more or less fine. I wasn't talking much, and I didn't eat, but my head wasn't pounding and I could see fine. I couldn't say the same for when night fell. It terrified me to sleep. I had the same dream three nights in a row, and each time I woke up in a cold sweat screaming my lungs out. Aunt Jasmine had to make me a sleeping potion just so I could get some shuteye, but it barely worked.

By the fifth day, Uncle Hesperus was going out of his mind with concern. Nightshade would stay by my side almost constantly, even though I told him that Sam and Melissa needed his protection more. I grew paler, and dark circles appeared, accentuating my icy blue eyes, and making me look like a complete zombie. In a way, I was.

The next night Nightshade tried to help by holding my hands in his, like he had done a couple of weeks ago. I felt calmer almost instantly, and while I was certain I would have the dream again, it didn't scare me as much. I kept his hand clasped in mine while I drifted off, afraid that without him as an anchor, the dreams would worsen.

I awoke feeling better than I had in days. My night was completely dreamless for once. Nightshade wasn't there when I woke up, so I pranced downstairs with a smile on my face, hoping to thank him.

I found Nightshade sitting on the deck. The early morning sun was just clearing the horizon, filling the sky with pastel hues of pink and purple. His lavender hair was tied up in a long ponytail, and his eyes were closed as he took deep breaths. The sun caressed his skin, making his tan more golden, and his pointed ears were on full display. The burn on his cheek was almost fully healed, leaving just the faintest trace of a pale pink scar.

He looked so peaceful that I started to go back inside, but his violet eyes opened just as I was about to turn around.

"Come join me," he said, his voice low.

I walked over and sat down cross-legged in front of him. His full lips turned up into a smile, and my heart skipped a beat.

"How did you sleep?" Nightshade asked.

"Better than I have in days." I whispered, not wanting to disturb the peace of the morning.

"I am glad. You look beautiful in the sunlight."

Heat crept up my cheeks, and my heart started pounding. Nightshade raised his hand to my face and slowly caressed my cheek with the back of his hand. I closed my eyes and leaned into his touch. Even after he took his hand away, the heat of his touch warmed my skin. I opened my eyes with a sigh, only to find Nightshade so close I could see little flecks of gold in his purple eyes. I leaned in closer until he was a breath away. He inhaled deeply, his eyes never leaving mine.

"You should go find Lady Jasmine," Nightshade whispered as he slowly pulled away, giving me room to breathe.

I stood up quickly and walked inside, trying to calm my breathing. The resounding rejection stung as I closed the door behind me.

I found Aunt Jasmine in her room getting ready for work. She was sporting a sleek ponytail and a brown leather jacket with jeans. Her usual librarian look. Her eyes widened when she saw me in the mirror.

"Hey there, lady! You're looking a lot better!"

"I feel a lot better. Actually, I was thinking of going to school today," I said.

She tugged on her ponytail. "You sure you don't want to stay home another day and get some rest?"

"I'm sure."

The last thing I wanted was to be home right now, especially when Nightshade's rejection was still so fresh. I headed up to my room and got changed. I pulled on jeans and a black sweater, and dashed out the door.

I saw Sam on the road to school and ambushed him with a hug.

"Whoa!" he yelled. "Your aunt said that you got sick. Are you okay now? You still look a little pale."

I flashed him a huge smile to show him how okay I was. He returned my smile, and we walked the rest of the way to school together. We caught up with Melissa before classes started and she, too, asked if I was okay. Did I really look that bad?

Melissa and I sat down in history, and that's when things took a turn. I started feeling woozy again, and the spots of light were back. Uncle Hesperus scrutinized me, frightened. I motioned I was fine. Halfway through class, though, I was not fine.

The headache grew, and the spots of light turned to images. Images of blood, red moons, and black swords. I wasn't even sure you could call what I did a scream. A sound so blood curdling erupted out of my mouth that nearby teachers ran into the classroom. Bits and pieces of reality peeked through the spots of images. The other kids in class looked shaken while in the vision, the moon was full, and the shadowed figure raced toward my friends.

Uncle Hesperus tried to calm them down and reassure the teachers who were coming into the room at the same time. He was also trying to make sure I was okay. It did not go well. Someone must have called 911 because paramedics came and rushed me to the hospital. The same images replayed over and over like my brain was on a loop. My head felt like it was about to explode, and according to the ER staff, I was bleeding out of my nose and ears.

A few agonizing hours and some morphine later, the spots were disappearing and my head felt less like a grenade. The hospital staff diagnosed it as a migraine—although they didn't sound sure—and told me I should go home and rest. Aunt Jasmine was in the waiting room and she stood up as I staggered over to her.

She wrapped me in a hug and whispered, "We're talking when we get home." Great.

Uncle Hesperus was already there when we got back to the house. He paced the living room, hands clasped behind his back and brow furrowed.

"What the hell happened?" he demanded, as Aunt Jasmine helped me onto the couch.

"I had the dream again, only this time, I was awake." My voice was hoarse from screaming. Aunt

Jasmine and Uncle Hesperus looked at each other and nodded.

"What you had was a vision," Aunt Jasmine explained. "Visions are very rare for witches. Unheard of, really."

"And very dangerous," Uncle Hesperus added.

"How dangerous?" I asked.

"You could die."

"Don't scare her." Aunt Jasmine lightly put her hand on Uncle Hesperus's shoulder.

"Why not? She should be scared. I sure as hell am." He smoothed back my hair with a gentle touch.

"Wait a minute. How could I die?" My heart picked up pace, and my hands trembled.

"Visions take a terrible toll on witches, both physically and mentally," Uncle Hesperus said. "The visions could cause your heart to stop or your brain to melt."

I nodded slowly. That was so not what I wanted to hear.

Uncle Hesperus made me a special potion at bedtime, one that would help with the headaches and the spottiness. None of us were sure why my visions were coming through in spots, but Nightshade had an idea.

"Maybe her visions are being sporadic because of the mark that you have placed on her arm," he suggested to Uncle Hesperus.

That was a thought. The mark on my arm was supposed to keep my magic in check. Keep it suppressed until I learned my lesson and Uncle Hesperus deemed my punishment over. But if normal visions caused my brain to pop, there was no telling what harm suppressed visions might cause me. I swallowed hard as I contemplated this, and Nightshade noticed. He sat down beside my bed and grabbed my hand. I squeezed so tight I thought I might break his fingers.

"The fact of the matter is, we have no idea why her visions come and go. The Mark of Sealing is a theory, but it's just that. I'm not taking the mark off unless and until we know more about what's going on. For now, the lessons will continue," Uncle Hesperus's tone was kind, but he was afraid. Maybe taking the mark off would make me die faster. I shuddered at the thought.

Since Uncle Hesperus wouldn't take the mark off until I had mastered what it meant to be a witch, we came up with a plan to increase the lessons. I huffed, but said nothing. This was the only way to get the mark off so I could be free of the intense pain the visions caused.

Aunt Jasmine took me out of school for the week, and all we focused on were the lessons. Rituals, history with humans, the origin of Amethystia, you name it. It was intense and tiring, but on the bright side, I was actually learning some new things.

One day, after a particularly arduous lesson about harnessing energy and how to do it safely, I went to the kitchen to get some water and noticed Uncle Hesperus using a scrying mirror to look at the what the spy bugs were seeing.

"Anything?" I asked. He jumped. That was new. Normally, nothing could surprise him.

"No," he said. "I don't think your friends are the witch hunters."

"Told you. So, can I take the larvae out of their houses and stop spying on them?"

He turned the scrying mirror over. "Do it tonight. There's nothing else for me to see."

An hour later, I knocked on Melissa's door, and her dad answered.

"Ebony, hello. Melissa isn't here right now. Is there something I can help you with?" Melissa wasn't home? Weird. She wasn't supposed to go anywhere else with the witch hunter still around.

"Is she at Sam's?"

"Not that I know of, but I can call."

I told him that wouldn't be necessary and walked back down the sidewalk. Where could she be? Nightshade had been very diligent in making sure that Sam and Melissa were okay while I couldn't be there. As I hurried home, I noticed a black car parked on the side of the road, near a bunch of trees and shrubs. I kept walking, but when I looked back, I stopped. That was the car that almost hit us! I knew because the license plate was custom. I jogged down the hill and heard faint voices. As

I got closer, I ducked behind a bush. It was dark in the woods, but I made out two—three figures. They all wore dark clothing.

"We can't kill her," one figure said. A woman. Her voice sounded familiar.

"Why not? She saw us. She'll tell the witches who we are," the second figure said. This one was male, but I didn't recognize his voice.

"Enough," the third figure said. This voice was male too, but more commanding. He was in charge. "The girl will not die today. She can be helpful."

I wanted to know who they were talking about. I moved closer.

"She saw me, my lord," the male figure said. "She'll report me."

"Well, there's an easy way to fix that," the one in charge said as he drew a blade from his side and sliced it across the other male's throat. I heard someone scream. It *was* Melissa! They had her!

"Now there's no one to report."

"My lord," the female said shakily, "the girl doesn't know our faces. Let her go to the witches. There's no evidence, and the witches will be scared."

"Not these witches. You don't know them like I do. They won't be scared off just because we kidnapped one of their own."

"So let me try to run over them again," she said. "It was fun seeing the look on that freak's face."

"While she's here listening to your plan?" the male asked.

My eyes widened. I clamped my hands over my mouth and tried not to make a sound.

"No, we'll let her take her friend home," he continued. "The real fun begins soon. Remember that, Ebony."

I didn't think my eyes could go any wider, but then the male opened a portal, and I thought my eyes would pop right out of their sockets.

I ran to Melissa as soon as they disappeared. They had tied her to a tree and gagged her. I untied the ropes and helped her up. She wrapped her arms around me in a vise grip. We approached the body lying on the ground.

He had to be only seventeen. His thick black hair curled around a pale face splattered with blood. I recognized him. I didn't know his name, but I knew he went to school with us. He was maybe a year ahead. I had seen him with Richelle a bunch, but I thought little of it until now. I grabbed Melissa's hand as I hauled her up the hill, explaining my theory.

We stumbled through the door where a frantic Aunt Jasmine greeted us. Melissa's dad had called, saying I had stopped by, and Melissa was nowhere to be found. He then called Sam's house, and Sam had called Aunt Jasmine freaking out because I wouldn't pick up my cell. I told her we were fine, but I didn't think we would be for long.

"What does that mean?" Uncle Hesperus asked from the corner he was standing in. I jumped. I hadn't seen him there.

I filled them in on what happened in the woods and my theory that Richelle was the other witch hunter. I had only heard Uncle Hesperus swear a few times, but never like this. He used words I wouldn't dare repeat to anyone.

Nightshade tried to calm him down, but that only made it worse. Melissa and I agreed it would be better if we spent the night elsewhere. That would give me an excuse to get the bug out of Melissa's house.

After dinner, and after we had filled Sam in on everything, we all sat around the TV in Melissa's basement, watching old reruns of cartoons and eating popcorn. Melissa curled up on the couch, staring off into space. She didn't even respond when I asked if she wanted more popcorn.

She excused herself to get changed, while Sam and I shared a worried look. I went out on the back patio for some fresh air, and Sam followed.

"It's chilly," he said, wrapping a blanket around my shoulders.

"I don't mind it. I like the cold."

Sam nodded absentmindedly. I gave him a curious look.

He cleared his throat. "I don't like you being in danger."

"I don't like that I put you guys in danger either."

"No, I mean, I don't like that you're in danger at all. I wish I could protect you."

"That's not your job, Sam."

He faced me. "I know it's not my job. I'm not your boyfriend. But I want to be."

I snorted. "My boyfriends don't protect me eith—wait, what did you say?"

"I said I want to be your boyfriend." Sam blushed and brushed a hair from my cheek.

I was speechless. Surely he didn't mean boyfriend, like *boy*friend. No. What he meant was a friend. That was a boy. Yeah. That was what he meant.

That was not what he meant.

As I stared at him dumbfounded and speechless, he leaned in and pressed his lips to mine. They were warm and soft. I was so shocked, I couldn't move. He noticed right away and broke the kiss.

"I'm sorry, I shouldn't have—" he started.

"No, it's not your fault," I said. "I just—I—"

I couldn't think of the words. I always had a fondness for Sam, but I didn't *like* him.

He nodded grimly, accepting what I couldn't say, and returned to the house, leaving me alone, and colder than I had ever felt before.

I went back inside, my mind still processing what had just happened. Sam liked me. He had *kissed* me. Melissa came back into the living room and noticed the change immediately. She looked between the two of us, but neither of us said a word. Tension filled the rest of the evening. Sam told us he wasn't feeling well and that he had to go home. Nightshade escorted him back to his house. I felt awful. I didn't know the correct way to handle this, so while Melissa and I were climbing into bed, I asked her.

"How do you deal with someone who is your friend, but they want more than you do?"

"That's a tough question." Melissa smiled wryly. "You're talking about Sam, right?"

"How did you...?"

"He's had puppy dog eyes for you ever since you came here."

"He has?" I asked, obliviously.

"Have you never had a boy yearn for you?" she asked incredulously.

"I mean, I have, but it's never been someone I'm close to." I hugged my knees to my chest.

"It's different when it's your friend." Melissa's voice was quiet—resigned.

"It is?" I asked.

Melissa nodded and turned away from me, pulling the covers over her.

"Wait, Melissa, do you... do you *like* Sam?"

She was quiet.

I sighed. "I didn't know."

"Neither does he," she said.

She didn't say any more, and I didn't ask any more. We just both fell asleep in the sad silence of boy trouble.

)) ● ((

I took the bug out of Melissa's house before we left for school. Neither of us ran into Sam all day, and I worried.

I was at my locker when Richelle passed by. Neither of us said a word. We just glared at each other. I waited for Sam to show up at the house after school, but he was a no-show. I called his cell and texted about twelve times. No response. So, I finally called his mother's cell, and she told me he wasn't feeling well.

I hung up the phone. It was all my fault.

I snuck out of the house and went to the park. Someone sat down next to me on my favorite bench. I knew who it was, but I wished it was Sam. I wanted to apologize.

"What brings you out here on this cold autumn evening?" Fabian asked.

"I wanted to know what it felt like to be an ice cream cone."

Fabian chuckled. "Well, if your ice cream ever feels like melting, I can help. We didn't exactly get to finish what we started earlier."

I knew I shouldn't. It would break Sam's heart if he knew. Then again, I already broke it, and mine needed fixing.

I grabbed his face and kissed him. Hard. He grinned against my mouth and kissed me back with just as much force. Fabian's lips were not like Sam's. Sam's lips had been soft. Fabian's were hard and unyielding. He took control of the kiss and grabbed my hands. He put them around his neck and his hands went around my waist. I couldn't get close enough to him. I straddled him on the bench and wrapped my arms tighter around his neck. His arms felt their way up my torso to my breast. He grabbed it harder than necessary, and it was like ice cold water had landed on me. I didn't want this. As hot as Fabian was, this wasn't what I wanted to happen. This wasn't who I wanted this to happen with. I pushed myself off him, breaking the kiss. We were breathing hard, and Fabian had a wild look in his eyes.

"What the hell?" he yelled.

"I can't. I'm sorry, I just can't."

His gaze turned from angry to furious. He got off the bench and slapped me across the face. I grabbed my cheek, stunned.

"You're a tease." His body went still and coldly detached.

I straightened my posture. "And you're an asshole!"

He smiled a cocky half smile and leaned in close to me. "If you think you're going to get away with that, you're wrong, bitch."

"Get. Away. From. Me," I said deliberately.

Fabian grabbed my upper arms and squeezed them tightly. "Or what?"

"She said get away from her!" Sam yelled as he ran to Fabian and knocked him over the head with a broken tree limb. Fabian grunted as his hold on me loosened. I wiggled out of his grasp and put as much distance between us as I could.

"Why you little—" Fabian said as he whirled on Sam. Sam needed help or Fabian would pulverize him. I still had the stupid mark on my arm, but I could do basic magic. I looked around frantically until I found a small stick. We weren't at Hogwarts, but I sure felt like Harry Potter as I picked it up and focused my magic into the tip of the twig.

"*Magicae!*" I yelled, and a blast of magic hit him in the back of the head with enough force to knock him out.

Fabian fell to the ground, unconscious, as Sam and I got the hell away before he woke up.

CHAPTER NINE

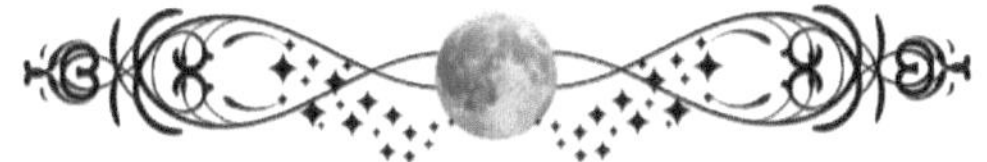

S AM AND I SAT on his bed in silence. I didn't know what to say. If he saw what happened between me and Fabian... well, that would've been an awkward conversation. So we just sat there, neither of us making the first move to talk. I focused on my breathing, listening to the fan whir. I tried to gather my thoughts enough to make a cohesive sentence.

"Sam..."

"I know," was all he said.

More silence. More breathing. Another attempt.

"You saw."

"Everything."

Damn it. I drew invisible doodles on the comforter.

"I'm sorry."

"Why? It's obvious you like him. And why wouldn't you? He's a bad boy. Aren't girls attracted to that?"

"Not anymore," I said.

Sam looked at me and raised an eyebrow.

"I had a boyfriend back home. He was a bad boy."

He scrunched his face up and shook his head.

"He's part of the reason I got exiled here. So no, I don't like bad boys anymore. They're much more trouble than they're worth."

"But you would never go for me," he said.

"I think Melissa sort of likes you."

Sam clasped his hands together. "Melissa? Our Melissa?"

I nodded and stood up.

"Huh." He rested his chin on his hands as he thought about what I just told him.

We awkwardly waved to each other as I left. Aunt Jasmine was waiting in the kitchen when I walked through the back door, her arms crossed and her "fake mom" look coming on strong.

"Why did you sneak out?"

"I was tired of being watched all the time."

"So, you wreaked havoc here and worried us all for fun?"

"It wasn't like that."

She raised her eyebrows higher and tapped her fingers against her forearm.

What was I supposed to tell her? That I snuck out so I could get hot and heavy in public witha boy I barely knew and when I said no, he forced himself on me?

She went to the sink and poured water into the glass she always used to clean her brushes.

"Make no mistake, you're still in trouble for tonight. But I have a painting to finish. Stay in your room."

I trudged up to my room, glad the nightmare day was over. Not like I wanted to go out right now. I got into my pjs, cuddled up in bed, and tried not to think about what had happened tonight.

☽ ☽ ● ☾ ☾

I woke screaming from the vision again, except this time, I knew exactly when everything would happen.

Aunt Jasmine, Uncle Hesperus, and Nightshade were in my room in a matter of minutes, and I told them the very important detail.

"A full moon?" Nightshade glanced at the night sky from the window.

I shook my head. "Not just any full moon. *The* full moon."

"You mean the one on Halloween." Uncle Hesperus leaned against the wall with his arms crossed.

He looked nonchalant, but his jaw was clenched. I nodded. Aunt Jasmine took a deep breath and ran her hands across her face.

The Halloween full moon was special because it was the one full moon that was the closest to the horizon. Halloween was kind of like Amethystia's New Year. Fireworks, festivals, and fun until the sun came up. The expressions on everyone's faces immediately made me regret telling them. They all looked grim, and even scared.

"Halloween is in two weeks," Aunt Jasmine said. Well crap. No wonder everyone looked terrified.

There was no way we could stop things before then. We didn't even know what exactly was going to happen. We decided it would be best to talk about this when everyone had gotten some sleep, so Uncle Hesperus and Aunt Jasmine went back to bed while Nightshade remained in my room.

"You are scared too," he whispered.

"I'm petrified," I whispered back, clutching the covers tightly. "These visions come to me, but they're not telling me what I need to know. They're not giving me anything."

"We now know that it is during Halloween."

"Big whoop. Who's doing this? Why are they doing this? That's what I want to know."

"And we will figure that out," he said, placing his hands over mine. "Together."

Nightshade put his arms around me and pulled me into his chest. He was warm. The smell of vanilla and musk was comforting. I snuggled closer and sniffled, tears blurring my vision. Why was this happening? Why did someone want to destroy the magical realm? Was it humans? We knew Richelle was working with a witch. Or at least we had a theory about it. I swallowed the tears back down. I didn't know what was going on right now, but I would find out.

I pulled out of Nightshade's grasp. I told him I was fine and he should go back to bed. He gave me a smile as he left my room, and that smile warmed me up from the inside. That smile gave me the courage to do what I needed to do tomorrow.

The next day after school, Aunt Jasmine and I were working as usual on my lessons. I was doing pretty good, too, until we began reviewing the rules witches were supposed to know about using magic.

"When is it acceptable to use magic on another witch?" Aunt Jasmine asked.

"When they don't know how to shut up," I answered. Aunt Jasmine gave me an exasperated look.

"Okay, let's try an easier one. When is it acceptable to use magic on a human?"

"When they're trying to kill you."

Aunt Jasmine sighed. "It's almost as if you don't want to get that mark off of you."

"Trust me, I do. I just don't see the reason I have to answer these stupid questions."

"Because these 'stupid questions' are the one thing stopping you from getting your magic back."

I knew she was right. This was the last step in proving I had "mastered" being a witch. I knew I had to take this seriously, or these visions would kill me faster than I wanted them to. Not that I wanted them to kill me at all.

"Maybe her vision was wrong?" Melissa chimed in, trying to be the optimist. "Maybe it was a different full moon, or maybe it was next Halloween."

She looked at Sam, and Sam shook his head sullenly. Her face fell.

"What does this mean for the human world?" Sam asked.

Personally, I had been trying to not think about that part. The human world had grown on me. I saw why Aunt Jasmine liked it here so much. I liked it here too, and I didn't want to see it in shambles.

When no one answered him, he just went back to his homework. None of us wanted to speculate about that.

I stalked into the entryway and grabbed my maroon jacket and my backpack.

"Where are you going?" Aunt Jasmine asked.

"Out." I flung open the door. I needed some air. And some caffeine.

The line at Presto Espresso was unimaginably long. I crossed my arms over my chest as I waited for my turn to order.

"Fancy seeing you here," Fabian said, sneaking up next to me.

The line moved inch by inch. Which was still too slow.

"Fancy seeing me? In the coffee shop I always frequent? Smooth. No offense, but I came here to be alone. No—actually—I mean all the offense in the world."

The line moved up another inch as Fabian chuckled. I rolled my eyes at his arrogant stance.

"I came here to be alone, too. Especially since my head still hurts," he said between clenched teeth.

"Poor thing. Maybe you should, like, leave and get it checked out?"

It was finally my turn in line. I ordered a white chocolate mocha and before I could hand the cashier the money, Fabian swiped his card through the machine.

"You can pay me back later." With a wink, he turned and exited the shop, leaving me with my mouth gaping at him.

I begrudgingly took my drink and sat in the usual booth in the back. I wrapped my hands around the warm cup and closed my eyes. Images of the full moon and blood filled streets swam through my head, only this time it wasn't part of the vision. I was trying to remember any little details I could. The sword that the hooded figure held in his hands popped into my head, clear as day.

I took a napkin from the table and pulled a pen from my bag. I scribbled the design of the sword, cursing when the thin material ripped in two from the pressure. The sword was important. I knew it. I just didn't know why. Every time I thought about it, I felt a tug inside my stomach, like my vision drew me to the sword.

I jumped when Nightshade slid into the booth across from me, his eyes full of sympathy.

"Why can't anyone leave me alone?" I thumped my head on the table.

"Because I am worried about you," he said. His voice was soft, like velvet washing over me.

I took a deep breath and opened my eyes. "Thanks."

"What were you drawing?"

I told Nightshade about the sword and the vision I had. Nightshade nodded and took the ripped napkin from the table, examining it. I saw him bite his bottom lip to keep from laughing.

"What's so funny?" I asked.

"It is not much to go on." He held up my poorly drawn sword.

It actually looked more like an amoeba than anything else. I busted out laughing, and Nightshade laughed with me. We were both in tears by the time our giggles stopped. Nightshade took my hand in his and my skin tingled at the contact. His face grew serious, and I tried to get him to tell me what was wrong. Nightshade looked me in the eye.

"Ebony Amberwood," he said, "I want you to know that I will fight by your side in this battle. If you want me to, I will be your protector, your ally, and your friend. I do not know what I would do if you somehow got hurt, but I am not too worried. You are a force to be reckoned with. I pity anyone who goes against you."

Heat flooded my cheeks, and I had to look away to keep tears from forming. When I looked back at Nightshade, his eyes were shining with warmth. I squeezed his hand in mine.

Nightshade's eyes glanced between my eyes and my lips. I leaned forward slowly, and I felt him lean in as well. We were a breath away when the most grating voice interrupted us.

"Isn't that cute? The freak has an even freakier boyfriend."

I leaned back and turned toward Richelle. I crossed my arms over my chest and tried not to show how excited I was at her calling Nightshade my boyfriend.

"You should watch your mouth Richelle. It might get you in trouble one of these days."

"Is that a threat, freak?" she sneered.

I looked her up and down. "You'll know when I'm threatening you. This is a warning. Back off."

Richelle leaned in close and spoke so low, I had to strain to hear her. "I'm not the one who needs to watch it, freak. You have no idea what I can do to you and your whole family. If you think for one second you can match me, then you have another thing coming."

"I think it is time for us to leave, Ebony." Nightshade said, scowling at Richelle.

He got out of the booth and held his hand out to me. I laced my fingers through his and brushed past Richelle. Her icy stare bore into us as we headed out the door of Presto Espresso.

Nightshade escorted Sam and Melissa home shortly after we returned to the house. Aunt Jasmine was busy painting in the living room. She took a sip of her wine and motioned me over.

"Sam seems different. Not as... infatuated with you. Did something happen?"

"Sam was never *infatuated* with me." I meandered over, the smell of the cinnamon candle burning filled my nostrils. "But some words might have been said."

"And those words were?" she asked.

"It doesn't matter. We're at an understanding now, I think."

Aunt Jasmine smiled. She threw her red wine at the canvas.

"What was that for? I liked that painting!" I shouted.

She laughed. "Have a look," she said in between giggles. "What does it say to you? How does it make you *feel*?"

I looked between her and the painting. "It makes me feel like I have a weird aunt."

She took a step back and squinted her eyes. "You might not be wrong there, but I see the wine on the canvas and I see... spontaneity."

"Really? Cause' all I see is a big blob of wine."

"That's because you're looking at the surface. Look within yourself and see the answer. It might not be conventional, but it will be right for you," she said.

"Are you drunk?" I laughed.

"Maybe a little, but I also have eyes... you and Nightshade looked pretty cozy when you got home."

Heat crept up into my cheeks. "Maybe. "

She peered at me from the corner of her eyes. "What kind of response was that?"

I shrugged, but my face felt like it was on fire. Aunt Jasmine wrapped her arm around me and kissed the top of my head.

"Don't be embarrassed. I like it. He's a decent guy, and he'll keep you safe, which is all I could ask for."

"Thanks."

I went upstairs and flopped onto my bed with a smile that wouldn't disappear.

I hatched a plan that night. The fight with Richelle wasn't over. The next day, it was back to business. Richelle wasn't in school, which was fine with me. She would see me soon enough. I walked through the day, playing the outstanding student, answering questions in class, but I was being anything but. I spied on Richelle's friends, finding out what their schedules were. If she wanted to see me as the wicked witch, then I would gladly oblige.

As one of her friends passed me to go to their next class, I "accidentally" bumped into them, dropping one of the spy bugs into their pocket.

After school it was the normal homework and witch lessons. Sam and Melissa left at their usual time, and I went to bed until the house was asleep.

When everything had been quiet for a while, I made my move. I got up and got dressed, grabbed the scrying mirror from Uncle Hesperus' nightstand—it was a vital part of the plan—and snuck out of the house. I was about to run down the street when a hand caught me by my forearm.

"Going somewhere?" Nightshade asked.

"How did you—"

Nightshade raised an eyebrow as if I should already know the answer to the question I was about to ask.

"You stalk me, don't you!" I whispered dramatically.

"I would call it being a bodyguard, since that is what I am."

"I would call it an invasion of privacy."

Nightshade sighed. "What are you going to do? Spy on Richelle's friend?"

I jutted my chin out. "No. If you must know, I was going to confront Richelle."

"The witch she is working with must have put protections up for that very thing, and the mark on your wrist limits your magic." Nightshade ran his fingers along my mark. My heart skipped a beat as I reveled in his touch.

"I don't need a reminder."

"No." Nightshade closed his eyes and took a deep breath. When he opened them again, I saw resolve. "What you need is an accomplice."

My face must have conveyed the shock I felt, because Nightshade chuckled.

"Yes, I will help you. I want nothing more than for my family to be safe back home... and for the people I care about here to be safe as well." His cheeks flushed a wine red, making his tan deeper.

I took a step back. He cared about me? My stomach did somersaults. I brushed it off the best I could and together we went to make my enemy pay.

꩜ ꩜ ● ꩜ ꩜

Richelle's house was simple to spot. It was the biggest one on the block, towering over

Nightshade and me as we looked up at the second story in awe.

Nightshade looked around for enchantments, shattering any he saw. Once he gave the all clear, the rest was up to me. I found an open window on the first floor and climbed through.

What I saw stunned me. State-of-the-art appliances and marble counter tops made up their vast kitchen. My mouth hung open as I took in the enormous chandelier above the dining room table. Nightshade had to whistle at me to get me to focus. I tore my gaze away and continued with my mission.

I walked carefully up to the second floor and found Richelle's room easily. It was the only door with a pink sparkly R hanging from it. I snuck in and closed the door behind me.

Richelle's sleeping form silhouetted against the moonlight coming through the window. Her breathing was even, and the rollers she put in her dark brunette hair were coming undone. I didn't know if I could go through with my plan. She didn't look like an evil mastermind—or even an evil minion. She looked like any other teenage girl, but I thought of how she put my family in danger and that steeled my nerves.

I clamped my hand over Richelle's mouth. She jerked awake. I put one finger to my mouth, signaling she should be quiet. Richelle nodded with eyes so wide I could see the whites of them in the dark, and I pulled my hand from her mouth so she could talk.

"What are you doing her, witch?" she spat.

"So you know. Good. I'm here because you're going to tell me who you're working for."

"Not a chance." She opened mouth to scream, but I quickly pulled out the scrying mirror.

"Oh, no you don't." I tapped twice on the glass, activating it. An image of Richelle's friend sleeping peacefully showed up on the reflective surface.

"Make any sudden movements, or cry for help, and your friend is burnt toast. Much like your backpack."

She looked at me in horror. The Seers' Larvae couldn't harm anyone, but she didn't know that. I asked her again who she was working for.

"I can't tell you," she said.

"Why not?" I asked.

"He'll kill me."

"I'll kill her."

Richelle panted, her eyes darting across the room, possibly hunting for a weapon. Clearly, she was terrified. Just what I was going for.

"I don't know his name," she said when she couldn't find a suitable sharp object within reach.

"But you know he's a witch."

Richelle nodded, her face tight. "He came to me because my family had been witch hunters dating back to the Salem Witch Trials. He didn't know that we stopped doing that decades ago. But he taught me how to find and hunt witches. He said they—you—were coming to invade us and make us slaves."

I snorted and rolled my eyes. Wow. Humans really believed anything they were told.

"What does he look like?" I asked her in a slightly less commanding tone.

"I don't know that either. He always has a dark hood covering his face. But he sounds old, like at least twenty-one."

I nodded. At least this was some information. "And his plan?"

"He wouldn't tell me all of it, just that it involved—" She clamped her mouth shut. So she did know something of interest.

"It involves what? Tell me or she's dead." I thrust the mirror in her face, giving her a good look at her sleeping friend.

"It involves a witch's blood under a full moon. Like another witch's, not his, and they have to give it willingly. That's all I know, I swear."

I nodded. I believed that's all she was willing to give up without some show of actual force, but I didn't believe that was all she knew.

I backed off and told her if she mentioned my presence to anyone, there would be consequences for her friend. As I was leaving her room, I pulled out the other larva from my pocket and dropped it on her floor.

CHAPTER TEN

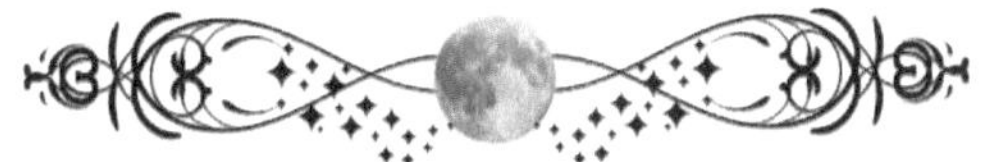

NIGHTSHADE AND I SAT on my bed as I recounted everything Richelle told me.

"You really believe she knows more than she is telling?" Nightshade asked.

To be honest, I didn't really know she was holding back anything, but that's what my gut was telling me. I nodded.

"It is a good thing you dropped the larva then," he mused.

"No kidding," I said as I lay back, my relief of having some answers turning into exhaustion.

Nightshade lay down beside me, his breathing evening out and my eyes slowly drifted closed.

The next morning, I awoke too hot next to a mess of purple hair. Nightshade had his arms draped over me and our legs tangled together under the sheets. We must have fallen asleep in my bed.

I marveled at his sleeping form. Long eyelashes framed his cheeks, and his mouth was slightly open. I reached out and ran my finger across his full lips. He stirred and sleepily opened his eyes.

"Good morning," he said.

"Morning." I smiled.

"We must have fallen asleep pretty quickly." He stroked my hair. I nodded, not wanting to let it slip that I enjoyed the feel of him around me.

He looked out the window and I followed his gaze. It was sunrise. Aunt Jasmine probably wasn't even up yet. The pink hue in the sky mixed with the blue to create a lavender color that reminded me of Nightshade's hair. He tightened his hold on me and I sank into him. His scent of vanilla and musk wrapped around me.

"The sunrise is beautiful today." I said.

"Yes, it is," he replied, but he wasn't looking out the window anymore. He was looking at me.

My gaze darted between his eyes and his lips. I wanted to kiss him. He looked at me with such intensity that I had a hard time breathing.

"Ebony." He said my name like a caress, his voice deeper than I've ever heard it.

We heard noise downstairs, and we jerked apart, even though no one else was in the room.

"I should go." He scrambled out of the bed.

Nightshade slipped out of my room, and I tried to get my breathing under control as I climbed out of bed. Once dressed, I headed downstairs for some coffee.

Before I reached the kitchen, however, I heard voices. I knew it was wrong to eavesdrop, but honestly, when did that ever stop me?

"She's not ready," Uncle Hesperus said.

"I disagree. I think she is ready."

"I'm not taking that mark off her until she learns—"

"Responsibility?" Aunt Jasmine finished for him, irritated. "She's more responsible than you give her credit for."

"She snuck out last night."

Aunt Jasmine sighed. "We don't know why she did that."

"Exactly! And until she can prove to me she can handle powerful magic, I'm not taking the mark off."

"She could die if you don't!"

"You mean die *faster*. Those visions will kill her over time, anyway."

"You are sentencing her to death because you want to feel in control," Aunt Jasmine bellowed.

"I *am* in control. It would behoove you to remember that," Uncle Hesperus said in a low, dangerous growl.

I had heard enough. I busted into the kitchen, startling both of them.

"How much did you hear?" Aunt Jasmine tugged at her sleek ponytail.

"Enough." I confronted Uncle Hesperus. "Aunt Jasmine is right. I've learned my lesson. Take the mark off me. Now."

"No."

"Do it, Hesperus," Aunt Jasmine commanded.

Uncle Hesperus sighed and stalked out of the room.

"He is so stubborn." I poured myself a cup of coffee.

She nodded and took a sip of her coffee. "I never thought he would put you in danger to make a point, though."

"Isn't there anything we can do? Can you take the mark off?"

Aunt Jasmine shook her head. "Only Hesperus can take it off."

"That sucks."

"Agreed. I have to get ready for work. We'll talk more later. Especially about why you snuck out last night." Aunt Jasmine put her mug in the sink and gave me a pointed look.

"It was for a good cause," I said.

"Mm-hm." She walked away, leaving me alone.

I sat in one of the chairs around the table and rested my head on my arms. Footsteps sounded outside, and then a knock on the front door sounded. I sighed and went to see who it was.

Sam and Melissa were over early today. They wanted to make sure I was doing okay. I assured them I was, and I suggested we go out for breakfast.

"That is not a good idea," Nightshade said, entering the foyer.

"Why not?" I asked.

"Remember the last time we went out for breakfast?"

I reminded him about last night and how I didn't think Richelle would try something so soon. He tried to argue, but I was already out the door.

We sat in our usual spot at Presto Espresso as I told Sam and Melissa what I had overheard this morning.

"That's so not fair!" Melissa crumpled her napkin.

"I agree," Sam said.

Of course, it wasn't fair. Uncle Hesperus knew the danger we were in, and he was still being stubborn.

Nightshade was silent as we ate breakfast. I couldn't tell if it was because I didn't listen to him about coming here, or if it was because he was thinking about this morning in bed. Either way, I reached over and squeezed his knee, silently telling him it was going to be okay. He smiled half-heartedly, although he never looked at me.

We agreed it was best that Aunt Jasmine knew about Richelle, so we headed to the library. There, I recounted what had happened the night before and I took out the scrying mirror. I placed it on the table and the mirror came to life, showing Richelle walking around her house.

"Cool," Melissa said, leaning over the mirror.

"Uh-huh." Sam agreed, almost bumping his head with hers.

Richelle went about her daily activities for about an hour, then the doorbell rang. The friend I had threatened last night was there and Richelle wrapped them in a big hug.

"I was so worried," Richelle said.

"About what?" her friend asked in confusion.

Richelle shook her head. There were tears in her eyes. "Nothing. I'm just glad to see you're okay."

"Of course I'm okay, you weirdo. Are you ready to go shopping or do you want to return to your home planet?"

"I'm ready. Just give me a sec." Richelle grabbed her bag, and I gasped when I saw what she put in it.

"What's up?" Sam asked.

"That's an athame," I whispered in fear. "And it's not just any athame either."

Richelle and her friend walked out the door, and the glass went dark.

"What's an athame?" Melissa asked.

"An athame is a type of knife used in rituals by witches," Aunt Jasmine said.

"She has—"

"I saw. A witch must have given it to her."

"Aren't you glad I snuck out last night?" I asked.

"No, but I am glad we have this information. We can use it to fight back." Aunt Jasmine rubbed her chin thoughtfully.

"What's going on?" Melissa asked.

I glanced at Aunt Jasmine, and she gave me a slight nod. "That athame is called Fangreaper. It poisons any witch that gets cut by it. The athame slowly steals their life essence and draws it into the blade," I said.

"That sounds... painful," Sam said.

"It is."

"What do we do?" Sam asked.

"You do nothing. You aren't the ones in danger," Uncle Hesperus said, walking toward us with Nightshade in tow. I hadn't even noticed my... friend left, but of course he would get my uncle.

"I know what we need to do," I said as I locked eyes with my uncle.

"Not here. Sam, Melissa, go home and do not go anywhere under any circumstances. Nightshade will escort you," Uncle Hesperus said.

Sam and Melissa complied without a word, and soon, they were out of sight. Uncle Hesperus sat down across from me with an annoyed gaze.

"I'm not happy that you snuck out—or that you stole my scrying mirror—but I am glad you came across this information. Keep watch. Memorize her schedule and when she's vulnerable, get that athame. No matter the cost."

"I agree we need to get out ahead of this, but Hesperus, I won't hurt her. She's just a kid. And human," Aunt Jasmine crossed her arms and sighed.

"I'm not saying hurt the girl, even though that would be the most efficient way to—"

"Hesperus."

"Fine. We won't injure the girl," Uncle Hesperus said. "But I want you to teach Ebony a memory wipe spell. I would do it myself, but I think it's less suspicious this way."

"She told me that her family were witch hunters dating back to the witch trials." I twirled a lock of hair through my fingers. "I don't think wiping her memory will do any good."

"We have to try," Aunt Jasmine said.

"Then let's get that mark off." Uncle Hesperus stood and walked away. Aunt Jasmine and I followed.

Once we were home—and I made sure that Sam and Melissa were okay—Uncle Hesperus took me out to the backyard.

"We're going to need some room for this," he said.

I rolled up my sleeve and held out my arm. Uncle Hesperus put his hand over the mark and muttered words so fast I didn't know what he was saying. My arm warmed and tendrils of light peeked through Uncle Hesperus' fingers as the mark glowed. I tried to pull away from the uncomfortable heat, but Uncle Hesperus held fast. Pain seared through my arm and I grunted. My whole body shook, and I wanted to collapse. The spots in my vision were back, showing me glimpses of the vision I kept having, but they melded together and the vision became clearer.

I saw shimmering water, black as night. Huge rocks hid the sword's location, and the sword itself was encased in gold. Uncle Hesperus said one last word in a language I didn't understand and the vision disappeared, returning me to the present. The last remnants of a light flashed as he released my arm and sunk to the ground.

I looked at my arm. The inky black swirls had vanished. I was free to do magic again. I looked down at Uncle Hesperus to thank him, but something was off. His skin was pale, and he was panting. I knelt next to him, but he brushed me off.

"It was... It was just a powerful spell, is all," he said in between breaths.

Aunt Jasmine and I helped him inside and laid him on the couch. I grabbed some water from the kitchen. He took it gratefully and gulped it down.

For the rest of the day, while Uncle Hesperus was recovering, Aunt Jasmine and I focused on the memory wipe spell.

"It's a very advanced spell, and most people don't even know how to cast it."

"Why not?" I asked as Aunt Jasmine and I walked outside.

"Because it's Soul Sorcery. I don't enjoy asking you to do this, but your uncle is too weak and I'm too scared to use it," Aunt Jasmine explained.

I swallowed hard. Soul Sorcery was the reason I had the mark put on. If they were asking me to use a forbidden magic, we must be in serious danger.

We studied the basics of how to cast Soul Sorcery—even though I already knew how—and then we moved on to the details of the spell. Aunt Jasmine pulled out a worn, leathery book and sat down in the grass. I sat down next to her and peeked over at the tattered, yellowed page.

"The human mind is resilient," Aunt Jasmine said. "This spell won't easily sway someone. That's why your opponent's guard should be down before you cast it. Preferably when they're unconscious." She turned the book so I could better.

"Like asleep?"

Aunt Jasmine tugged on her ponytail. "It won't be that easy, though. If the witch she's working with knows about our plan, they'll put protections in place. They probably already have."

"So just sneaking in and casting the spell while she's in bed won't work," I said.

"No, it won't."

"So, we have to fight. And knock her out."

Aunt Jasmine nodded reluctantly. We went over the steps of how to cast the spell. The moves my hand would need to make, and the words I would need to say. Aunt Jasmine didn't want me actually casting the spell until I had to, so we did those two things separately.

I had gotten the hand movements down when Uncle Hesperus walked over to us.

"How are you feeling?" I asked.

"Better. You look like you've got the hang of this."

I nodded. He smiled, but it didn't reach his eyes. I realized he didn't like this any more than Aunt Jasmine or I did. He forbade Soul Sorcery for a reason, and as king of the realm, he knew the risks of asking me to use it. If anyone found out, they would dethrone him. We practiced for about a half hour more and called it quits after that.

While getting some water, Aunt Jasmine suggested I call Melissa over to have a girls' night. I smiled widely and rushed for my phone. Melissa squealed and said she'd be right over. I told her to wait for Nightshade to escort her. She huffed, but ultimately agreed.

Thirty minutes later, Nightshade returned with Melissa in tow, and she wrapped me in a hug.

"How's everything going?" she whispered in my ear. I gave a slight nod, signaling everything was fine.

Aunt Jasmine shooed the boys out of the house for the night, and the three of us sat on the deck and painted while eating chips and salsa. Another thing I loved from the human world.

"Painting is so relaxing," Melissa commented as she slapped her brush onto the canvas.

"That's why I love it." Aunt Jasmine took a drink of wine while she contemplated her next stroke.

"Where's that?" Melissa asked, looking over at my canvas.

"What do you mean?" I had barely been paying attention.

I focused on my painting, and I dropped my paintbrush. Aunt Jasmine looked over and paled. I had never been good at painting, but on my canvas was a perfect recreation of Amethystia. My home. Only it wasn't my home anymore. It looked like a scene out of a dystopian movie. The trees were bare and decimated buildings littered the landscape. It was my vision. In color. On canvas. Tears welled up, and I grabbed the painting off the easel. I threw it in the air.

"*Ignis!*"

It immediately burst into flames as it fell to the ground. Aunt Jasmine rushed over and stomped out the fire before it combusted the leaves on the ground and we had a major fire. Melissa wrapped me in a hug, and I started crying. Why was this happening to me?

After the painting incident, we agreed it would be a good idea just to watch movies and relax. So that's what we did. I wasn't paying attention, though. I just thought of how close Halloween was getting. It was eleven days away, and we had yet to figure out a plan to stop my vision from coming true or what it meant. Of course, we didn't know the witch who employed the witch hunters was, and Uncle Hesperus had no luck finding out either. I hugged my knees to my chest as I contemplated the coming horrors.

After the second movie was over, we went to bed. Melissa and I had school tomorrow, after all.

I was lying in bed watching the fan blades spin when Melissa turned to me.

"Where was that in your painting?" she asked.

"Home."

"It's... pretty."

I gave her an annoyed looked and stared back at the ceiling.

"That was your vision, wasn't it?" she asked after a minute.

I nodded.

"I'm sorry," she said, upset, and rolled back over.

I sighed. "No, I'm sorry. I'm just freaked out, is all."

Melissa patted my back. "I bet."

I took a shaky breath. "Halloween is so soon, and I don't know what's coming or how to stop it."

"We'll figure out a way," she said with so much bravado it was hard to doubt her. However, the danger was undeniable.

"There's no *we* in this," I told her. "It's too dangerous. You and Sam will not witness any of that."

"Haven't you learned by now that the three of us are friends? Sam wouldn't let anything happen to you and neither would I. We are a team. So there most definitely is a *we*."

I still didn't think it was a good idea, but I smiled at her stubbornness. Melissa never gave up.

"Fine," I said, "there is a *we*. But you two are going nowhere near a fight."

"Fine." She looked like she wanted to say something else.

"Yes?" I prodded.

"Sam asked me out," she said sheepishly.

"What? That's amazing!"

She blushed as she nodded.

"I just... I feel like he asked me out because you turned him down."

"I doubt that's the case," I said. "You're gorgeous and funny and he would be a total loser if he didn't see that."

"You think?"

"I know."

Melissa took a sip of water sitting on the bedside table and beamed "So what about you?"

"What about me?"

"I noticed the way you looked at Nightshade in the library. You're totally into him."

"I am so not," I said, a little too defensively.

Melissa raised an eyebrow. I thought back to the café and the deck. Nightshade took my breath away and made me feel like I was breathing pure oxygen all at the same time. He gave me butterflies whenever I saw him. My skin tingled at his touch, and I got lost in his beautiful eyes so much that sometimes I didn't think I could find my way back to reality.

"I so am," I conceded with a groan.

"I knew it." Melissa squealed. "Have you kissed him yet?"

"No." My cheeks flushed with heat.

I'd actually thought about kissing Nightshade frequently. I dreamed of how his lips would feel on my mouth and neck. The heat spread down my neck and rested at my chest.

"Are you going to?" she pressed.

"I don't know!"

"Do you want to?"

"Melissa!"

We giggled. For the rest of the night we talked about boys and, for a moment, I forgot about the peril that lurked just in front of us.

CHAPTER ELEVEN

NIGHTSHADE RETURNED TO THE house while Melissa and I were eating breakfast. We stared at Nightshade, at each other, and back at Nightshade before we busted out laughing. He looked at us in confusion at first, but his lips curved up into a smile and his eyes softened. Aunt Jasmine shuffled into the kitchen.

"You girls look like you're having fun."

We smothered our giggles and continue eating. She shrugged and grabbed a cup of coffee. Uncle Hesperus limped into the kitchen and the mood immediately changed. Something was wrong. His skin was too pale, and a thin sheen of sweat glistened on his face.

"My king," Nightshade said, "what is wrong?"

"The witch hunter... she ambushed me last night. Used Fangreaper. Help."

I felt the color drain from my face. No. She wouldn't. She couldn't have. Uncle Hesperus took off his long navy-blue coat and I gasped.

Blood surrounded a rip in his shirt, and a stab wound was visible on the right side of his body. She really used the athame on him. I sunk to the ground, my knees banging against the hardwood floor. This couldn't be happening. She poisoned him. She killed him.

The entire room was silent. Even the sizzling of the bacon seemed to quiet down.

My uncle's labored breathing sounded raspy, and his lips held no color at all. He was already dying. This was unforgivable. I would make Richelle pay for what she did.

I rose from the floor and stalked to my room. Nightshade followed me.

"What are you doing?" he asked.

"I'm going to make her pay," I said as I got some clothes out of the closet.

"That is not wise."

"I don't care." My body shook, and I couldn't tell if it was from fear or rage.

Nightshade came up behind me and turned me toward him.

"Please, do not do this. Not while you are angry. She is human. She did not know what she was doing," he said desperately. "If you kill her, there is no going back."

I shook him off. This was not his decision. Richelle and I had been playing with each other until now, but this crossed the line. This was now war.

Nightshade grabbed my arm and pulled me to him. I wanted to push him away, but I made the mistake of looking into his eyes.

They were full of fear. He feared for me. And it wasn't just as a bodyguard. His hands burned my skin where they touched me, and he glanced between my eyes and my mouth. I took that as a sign. I grabbed his face between my hands and pulled him to my lips.

Everything in my body lit up. It was like Nightshade magnified every touch. His hands brushed up my arms, and I shivered as they held my face just as mine held his. His lips were soft against mine. Commanding, yet submissive. My face felt like it would combust from the heat.

I broke the kiss, remembering what I needed to do, although it was hard to remember anything with Nightshade still just an inch from my lips. I couldn't get enough air into my lungs. And judging by his breathing, he felt the same.

"Please," he begged.

I didn't know if he was asking for another kiss, or if he was still trying to stop me from confronting Richelle. It didn't matter. I wouldn't listen to either request.

I pushed him out of my room and closed the door swiftly, trying hard not to slam it. I changed into jeans and a tight black turtleneck, and I went back downstairs.

Everyone stared at me with a mix of emotions on their faces. Almost everyone. Nightshade wouldn't make eye contact with me. Melissa's face was pale and she had tears in her eyes while Aunt Jasmine bit her lip. Uncle Hesperus just looked like death.

Aunt Jasmine left the kitchen and returned holding something long wrapped in deep purple velvet

"Hesperus gave this to me when he first arrived here." She unveiled the object. It was a sword and its beautiful sheath had intricate gold patterns engraved into the dark leather. "He said to only use it if we were in severe danger. And I guess this counts, but don't use it unless you absolutely have to."

She handed the sword to me, and I unsheathed it. The metal glowed bright silver, and an etching of runes trailed up the blade.

"Those runes will guide your hand," Uncle Hesperus said weakly. He leaned heavily against the doorframe. "It will help you in whatever way you need. Trust in the magic, and trust in yourself."

I nodded and returned the sword to its sheath. I turned to Melissa.

"Call Sam and get him over here now. Before he leaves for school. And whatever you two do, stay here."

Melissa nodded.

"I will accompany you," Nightshade walked up to me.

I immediately shook my head. I wouldn't let Richelle hurt him again. "I need to do this alone."

"But—"

"Richelle won't hesitate to kill you. But *maybe* she'll hesitate with me."

"Don't count on that," Aunt Jasmine warned. "She's a witch hunter. It's her job to kill you. Just remember the spell and you'll be fine."

I nodded and hugged her tightly. She hugged me back just as fiercely.

We let go, and I stared at the faces of the people I cared about, committing them to memory, knowing I wasn't facing Richelle completely alone. I whipped around and stormed out of the house to confront the girl who had tried to take that away.

I stood in the school's parking lot, waiting for Richelle's car to show up. My phone dinged, and I let out a small breath of relief. Sam had arrived at the house. At least everyone would be safe when this went down. I had it all planned out. I would lead Richelle to the wooded area behind the school, far enough away so no stragglers would get in the way. Then I would swiftly kick her ass.

Richelle's car entered the parking lot, and my heartbeat picked up. I knew how to fight. I knew how to use magic. Why was I scared?

Richelle and her friend got out of the car and as they were walking toward the building, she stiffened. She turned around and glared straight at me. I straightened my posture and motioned with my head for her to follow me. She said something to her friend, then headed my way. Showtime.

I marched toward the forest. She was about ten paces behind me when I stopped in the middle of some thick trees and faced her.

"What do you want?" she asked.

"You stabbed my uncle," I said simply.

"So?"

"So?" My fists tightened at my sides. "He's going to die because of you!"

"Die? Look, I just stabbed the guy in the gut. He wasn't even bleeding that badly. I just did what I was told." Her face scrunched up in confusion.

"That knife you have poisons witches. It poisons our magic. Magic is like blood for us. It runs through our veins. The magic from that knife slowly shuts the body down."

Richelle balled her fists at her side. "Look, I didn't mean any harm—"

"Yes, you did. You knew exactly what you were doing." I widened my stance, getting ready to fight. "And now, it's time that you learned what dealing with witches is really like."

I thrust out my arms, palms out, and yelled, "*Magicae!*"

A burst of magic flew toward Richelle, she soared backward, hitting a tree. She got to her feet shakily and grabbed the athame out of her purse.

"You witch!" she yelled as she ran toward me. I dodged her easily and kicked her in the back, sending her tumbling in the dirt. How she managed to stab my uncle, I didn't know. She was weak and clums—

She recovered quickly and swiped her leg under my feet. I fell backward onto the hard ground. Ow. Okay. So, she knew how to fight, too. I leaped to my feet. I yelled and bent my body backwards as she swiped Fangreaper in the air where my head had been. She swiped again, and I couldn't keep my balance. I stumbled over a log and fell to the ground, hitting my head against the trunk of a tree. Stars rocketed through my vision, and my head throbbed. I felt warmth trickle down. I was bleeding.

She yelled again, and I rolled to the side as she stabbed the air. Murderous rage shone in her eyes, and I backed up as far as I could.

My back hit the trunk of another tree and I thrust my hand out toward Richelle.

"*Ignis sphaera!*"

A ball of fire formed in the air in front of my palm, and I hurled it toward Richelle. She ducked, and it hit a nearby branch, scorching it.

Okay, so maybe throwing fireballs in the forest was not the brightest idea I ever had, but it worked as a distraction. As Richelle was looking back at the damage I had just done, I scrambled to my feet and landed a kick to her gut. She stumbled backward, dropping the athame and clutching her stomach. She ran toward the knife, but I was quicker. I grabbed the handle and immediately cried out in pain. I let go of the athame, my skin bubbling and blistering from where I had touched Fangreaper. My palm smoked, the smell putrid. I stumbled back as I tried to stop the stinging pain.

"Fascinating, isn't it?" Richelle picked up the athame and turned it in her hand. "A witch says a few words over a silly knife, and any other witch who touches it gets burned. Kind of poetic, in a way. I mean witches. Burning. It's funny."

She prowled toward me. My hand shook from the pain. I tried to lift it, but every move was like fire. I whimpered as I crawled backward, trying to put as much space between us as possible. When I couldn't go any farther, I dug my hand into the earth. The cold from the earth soothed the pain a little. Richelle closed in, and I flung the dirt in her face, making her fall backward. I ignored the pain in my hand the best I could and unsheathed the sword hanging from my side. The blade gave the forest a magical glow, and the runes seemed to hum in tune with my magic. Richelle looked at the sword and her eyes widened in fear. I prowled toward her.

"Fascinating, isn't it?" I said, mimicking her voice. "A witch carves a few runes on a sword and the blade destroys anyone in its path. Kind of poetic, in a way. I mean humans. Being nothing. It's funny." I didn't know exactly what the runes did, but Richelle didn't need to know that. Uncle Hesperus said the runes would guide my hand, though, so I was hoping I was right.

Richelle screamed as I swiped the sword in the air, backing against a tree. With a cruel, manic smile, I crept a few steps closer and swiped the sword again. This time, I connected with Richelle's cheek. She yelped and clutched her face.

"You lose." I said, lifting the sword in the air.

Tears streamed down her face, and she looked like the poor rich girl she was. She hunkered down on the forest floor. My hand hovered in the air, wanting to strike, but my body wouldn't let me.

I couldn't kill her.

She sentenced my uncle to death, but I couldn't do the same to her. Nightshade's words echoed in my head. He was right. If I killed Richelle, there would be no going back. I would be a murderer. And I wasn't that. I wasn't like her. Sheathing the sword, I turned my back to walk away, and that's when it all went to hell.

I heard Richelle get up and rush toward me. My hand flew to the hilt of the sword, but I was a second too late. She jumped on my back and grabbed my hair. My throbbing head pounded. I tried to throw her off of me, but she held fast. I ran toward a tree and shoved my back against it. Richelle fell to the ground, some of my hair dangling from her fingers. I drew the sword and swung, but she was already standing. Richelle waved Fangreaper wildly. It took all my concentration to dodge her strikes. I fell over a tree branch, and pain rang in my tailbone as my butt hit the ground. Richelle still weilded the athame wildly, and she tripped over the same branch. She fell to the ground, but was quick to recover. She rolled on top of me and plunged the athame down. Instinctually, I brought the sword up at the same time. I heard a sickening squish.

Richelle's eyes widened as she gasped for air. She looked down at the same time I did and I shrieked. The sword had pierced Richelle in the chest. Blood trickled from her mouth and dripped onto my face. I couldn't move. My limbs were like ice. Cold, and frozen in place. Richelle stopped breathing and went limp, her lifeless eyes staring a hole straight into my soul.

☽ ☽ ● ☾ ☾

I didn't know how long I stayed there looking into Richelle's glassed over eyes, but after a while I heard yelling. Crap. The humans must have heard the noise and were coming to investigate.

I had to move, but my hands just held the hilt of the sword like it was the only thing keeping me grounded. The dew from the cold, hard forest floor seeped into my skin.

The weight of Richelle's body lifted off me, and someone helped me sit up. I didn't know who, though. Probably the police. They wrapped something warm around my shoulders, and I felt pressure around my body, like someone hugging me. I didn't even react. All I kept seeing was Richelle's face twisted in pain.

Someone knelt in front of me and tried to make me focus. They were saying something. Probably how messed up I was and how I was going to jail for the rest of my life. The person gently shook my shoulders. I didn't even blink. I felt the ground fall out from beneath me, and almost in an instant, I was inside. My feet weren't moving, but my body bobbed like I was walking. After a minute, I felt something soft underneath me, and something even softer cradling my head. I felt even more pressure on me, sinking me further into warm comfort.

⟩ ⟩ ● ⟨ ⟨

When my world came back into focus, it was dark outside. There were three heavy blankets on top of me as I lay on the couch in the living room. I tried to move, but my entire body was sore. I grunted and tried to sit up again, but gentle hands pushed me back down.

"Not yet," Nightshade said.

His face was kind. It shouldn't have been. I was a monster. Tears welled up in my eyes, and I started sobbing as I remembered what happened. He rubbed his hands over my covered arms, soothing me. I cried harder as he made gentle shushing sounds. He rose from his chair and left. Good. He shouldn't have been trying to make me feel better.

After a few minutes, he returned with a cup in his hands. He sat down and told me to drink it. I shook my head. Tea was the last thing I wanted right now. I just wanted to be left alone.

He told me that his was his people's remedy for grief. He said it wouldn't get rid of it, but it would lessen the blow. I shook my head again. I wanted to feel the grief. Someone died because of me.

After a few more minutes of Nightshade sitting with me, trying to convince me to drink the potion, he left. Aunt Jasmine took his place. I closed my eyes. I didn't want to see the disappointment I knew she felt. She wanted me to be good. But I wasn't. I wasn't good at all.

"Ebony," she said after several minutes of silence. I ignored her. She sighed.

After several failed attempts to get a reaction out of me, she, too, left. I was alone. Just where I deserved to be.

I cried for several more hours after that. The sun was rising when the tears finally dried up. I sat up, despite my body's protests. Every step hurt. Blackness surrounded my vision a few times, but I kept on going until I reached the kitchen. Aunt Jasmine was making coffee when she turned around and looked at me.

"Oh, sweetheart." She walked over and pulled me into a hug. The pain made me grunt, and she immediately released her hold on me.

"Want some tea?" she asked gently.

I nodded.

She helped me sit in one of the chairs and went to put the kettle on the stove, then sat down beside me as we waited for the water to boil.

"Where are Sam and Melissa?" I finally asked, my voice hoarse.

"They went home," she said.

I nodded. Good. I didn't want them to witness my weakness.

"And Uncle Hesperus? How is he?"

Aunt jasmine smiled. "The stubborn old man is just fine."

"How?"

"When Nightshade brought you back from the forest, he also brought Fangreaper back."

"But we can't use it. The spell—"

"Nothing a little hex reversal couldn't fix."

I nodded. Good. Uncle Hesperus was going to be fine. Unlike...

"She's dead."

Aunt Jasmine's smile disappeared. She didn't say anything. She just nodded.

"I killed her."

"You had no choice." Aunt Jasmine put her hand on my shoulder.

"But I did."

"I know you, Ebony. You wouldn't have killed her if there was another way."

Tears welled up once more, and I swallowed hard. I had a choice. I could've let her kill me. She should've killed me. It would have been better than feeling like this.

Nightshade walked into the kitchen and sighed with relief when he saw I was off the couch.

"How are you feeling?" he asked as he sat down on my other side.

"Like crap."

He stroked my hair. "Would you be willing to give the grief potion another chance?"

I nodded. He gave me a half smile and went to fix it.

"What happened to R—the body?" I asked.

Nightshade and Aunt Jasmine shared a look.

"We... made it look like a car crash." Aunt Jasmine's voice broke.

A car crash. Such a simple thing. People die from those every day.

Nightshade put a cup of swirling herbs in front of me. I tried to smile, but it wouldn't reach my eyes. I sipped the liquid, and the grief subsided little by little. By the time I finished the cup, I could think clearer.

"I have to go to school," I said.

"Not today." Aunt Jasmine gently pushed me back down into the chair. "Today you rest."

My shoulders slumped, grateful that I didn't have to put on a show.

"Why don't we watch some movies?" Aunt Jasmine suggested.

We filled the rest of the day with distractions, and I eventually felt okay. Sam and Melissa even came over after school and helped me finish the schoolwork I missed. By the time they left, I thought I was going to be alright.

CHAPTER TWELVE

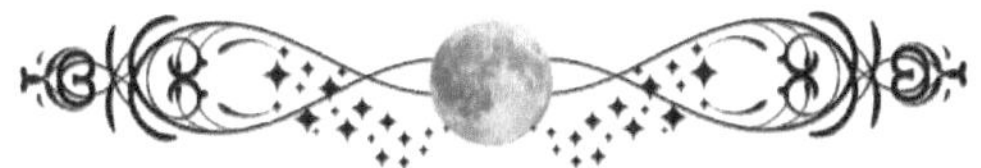

I WAS WRONG. THAT night, I woke up crying, trying to get the image of Richelle's glassy, distant eyes out of my head. It was dark, and the streetlights outside were the only thing illuminating my room. I looked around frantically, hoping I wouldn't see Richelle's ghost. When the room was empty, I let out a small sigh.

My door opened, and I gasped. I only relaxed when I saw it was Nightshade.

"Hey." I said, my voice hoarse.

"I thought I heard you." He sat down on the edge of my bed and brushed some hair from my face.

"I had a bad dream."

He continued to smooth my tangled hair. "Going through something like that... it is difficult. When I found you, you were lost. I could not get to you, and I did not think you would find your way back. After seeing you today, though, I know you will. It will just take time."

"Time that we don't have," I countered.

"I will lend you strength whenever you need."

I gave him a half smile. "You know what I need right now?"

"Hm?"

"I need you to kiss me."

Nightshade's hand paused, and he smiled. He then moved his hand to cup my cheek and pressed his lips gently against mine.

My whole body sparked to life. I kissed him back hard, and I sat up, making it easier to wrap my arms around him. He returned the passion, his hand moving from my cheek to the back of my head, holding me closer. I winced where he touched my wound, and he broke the kiss immediately. He rested his forehead against mine and cupped my cheek.

"That was..." I couldn't think of words.

"Intense," he said.

Nightshade pulled back, but my arms kept him right where he was.

"What's wrong?"

"You need sleep," he said. "And I do not think I am helping you relax."

"No, I'm very relaxed. Relax me some more." I batted my eyelashes.

Nightshade pulled back again and this time I let him, albeit with a pout on my face. Nightshade laughed and kissed my forehead.

"Get some sleep, Ebony."

"Will you stay with me tonight?"

Nightshade nodded and briefly left the room. Where was he going? He returned with a chair from the kitchen. He positioned it at the foot of my bed and sat down.

"That's not what I meant."

"I know what you meant. And it is not a good idea for me to be in bed with you."

I sighed. He was probably right, but that didn't stop me from sticking my tongue out at him.

He smiled in response. I lay back down and curled up under my covers. I fell asleep knowing nothing would come for me while Nightshade kept watch.

I woke up and could barely move. My muscles ached and my head pounded like I was at a nightclub. Nightshade moved to the edge of my bed and helped me sit up.

"Good morning," he said. I could tell he was worried about me. I brushed him off and sat back, leaning against the headboard.

"Morning," I said groggily.

"You are adorable when you first wake up." Nightshade brushed some of my ratted hair away from my face.

I gave a small laugh and groaned. Even laughing hurt. I tried to get up, but Nightshade said it would be best if I stayed put. I shook my head.

"I have school today," I said.

"Would it not be better if you stayed home?"

I shook my head again and tried to get up once more. This time, Nightshade held out his hands and helped me stand. The room spun and

I would have collapsed if Nightshade hadn't been supporting most of my weight.

"Now I know it would be better if you stayed home."

"I skipped yesterday."

Nightshade looked like he wanted to protest, but nodded and helped me to the living room, where Aunt Jasmine and Uncle Hesperus were arguing about the use of blue in one of Aunt Jasmine's paintings.

They stopped when they saw me, and Aunt Jasmine rushed over to help Nightshade get me to the couch.

"How are you feeling today?" Aunt Jasmine asked.

"Okay," I answered.

Aunt Jasmine raised her eyebrow like she didn't believe me. I wasn't sure I believed me either. Uncle Hesperus fumbled around in the kitchen, and my stomach immediately grumbled.

"I will go get you some food," Nightshade said and disappeared.

Aunt Jasmine and I just sat, looking at each other.

"I'm not exactly sure what to say," she admitted.

"There's nothing to say."

"You did what you had to."

I looked away and twisted a lock of hair between my fingers. "Doesn't make it any better."

Nightshade and Uncle Hesperus returned with a plate full of food. I ate some of it, but mostly, I just picked at the omelet.

All three of them watched me with guarded expressions. I stopped eating and looked right back at them.

"Can I help you guys?" I asked with as much sarcasm as I could. They continued to stare with worried faces. I rolled my eyes and picked at another bite. The doorbell rang and I got up as fast as my aching body would allow to answer it.

Sam and Melissa rushed in and hugged me when I answered the door. My body screamed with every touch.

"Are you okay?" Melissa took a step back and assessed me from head to toe.

The only thing I could do was nod.

"What happened?" Sam grabbed my hand and squeezed gently.

I shook my head. Looking at my two best friends' distressed faces made my eyes water. I didn't want them to worry about me.

"Are you coming to school today?" Sam asked.

"Yeah," I said. "Let me get dressed real quick. I'll be right back."

After I had brushed my hair, taking care of the knot at the back of my skull, and dressed in some warm clothes, I grabbed my backpack and headed downstairs.

Everyone was in the entryway, looking cautious. I insisted I was fine and went to face the consequences of my actions.

I didn't realize how difficult being at school would be until I actually came face to face with Richelle's locker.

Flowers and candles littered the area, with a large photo of her in the center. I choked back tears as I tried not to look at the shrine.

Classes were just as hard, as every teacher made their way around the room asking the students to share a memory of Richelle. I always skipped my turn.

Lunchtime was hell. Everyone was talking about the "accident" and theories flew. Everything from drunk driving to a conspiracy theory about someone out to get her made their way around the cafeteria. If only they knew that the conspiracy theory was the closest to how she actually died.

After classes, Sam and Melissa waited for me at my locker. They wore the same concerned expressions they had this morning. I once again told them I was fine, and we left the building.

My muscles relaxed as we got further from school. I hadn't realized just how tense I had been the entire day. All that tension returned when I heard a rustling in the bush behind us. I stopped and turned around. Nothing was there. Sam and Melissa stared at me with questioning looks. I just shook my head, and we kept walking.

The leaves brushed against each other again. This time, I didn't turn around, and instead I walked slower. Quieter. I heard the rustling again. I grabbed a stick from the side of the road and investigated the bush. Nothing. I shuffled back to my friends.

I didn't get to them though. The leaves rustled even louder, and I turned back to the bush when a blur of tan fur jumped at me. I raised the stick in self-defense, and huge fangs clamped onto the wood. I screamed and fell back. The creature kept chomping at the stick, breaking off huge chunks. I tried to shake it off, but the creature was too strong.

Something hit the monster. It yelped and turned its attention to its new target. I clambered to my feet, and I saw the creature fully for the first time. It was the size of a lion, with a lean body, and long, nasty claws. Its fur stuck out everywhere, and its tail flicked in irritation. I couldn't see its face, but I knew it would have four enormous eyes and a long snout. This creature was a Jaramoth, and it had its sights set on Sam.

I couldn't move. This creature was one I've only ever heard of. As a tracker, it wouldn't stop until it killed its target. I had killed Richelle. I was the target.

The creature stalked toward Sam while he backed away at the same pace. Melissa froze with fear. I couldn't say I blamed her.

Sam was dead if I didn't do something. I tried to summon a fireball, but my voice wouldn't work. I couldn't even raise my arm.

The creature lunged at Sam and scraped its claws against his chest. I screamed. Melissa screamed. Sam screamed.

Nightshade raced toward us at lightning speed and kicked the creature in the face. It yelped and turned its sights away from Sam. Melissa ran toward him. I could see a lot of blood. Melissa cried as she put pressure on his wounds. Nightshade attacked the Jaramoth and didn't stop punching and kicking it until it gave up and bolted off.

Nightshade ran to Sam. He nearly pushed Melissa out of the way and started mumbling something. His hands glowed with a warm yellow light as they hovered over Sam's chest. Sam didn't move. Nightshade was getting frustrated.

Distraught, Melissa dashed over to me and shook my shoulders. I didn't take my eyes away from Sam and Nightshade. Melissa screamed at me, but I didn't really hear what she was saying. She shook me harder, her nails digging into my skin. I didn't care. I couldn't make my body move.

At one point, I think she slapped me, but I wasn't sure. I just noticed Nightshade pick Sam up in his arms and run toward the house. Melissa gave up trying to get my attention and ran after them, leaving me standing in the street.

I finally remembered how to move, but all I could manage was a slow walk. My leaden feet dragged me to the house and through the front door.

Once I got there, everything was already in motion. Aunt Jasmine and Uncle Hesperus were binding Sam's wounds with gauze and Nightshade was tending to Melissa, trying to calm her down. I trudged upstairs and sat on the edge of my bed.

The Jaramoth had gravely injured Sam and I couldn't even cry. I just sat on my bed and repeated the words over in my head. Sam got hurt. Sam got hurt. That mantra slowly turned into, I hurt Sam. I hurt Sam.

The sun was lowering past the horizon when there was a knock on my door.

Aunt Jasmine sat beside me and put her hand on mine. It was still bloody from trying to keep Sam alive. All I could say to her was, "I hurt Sam."

We sat there for what seemed like hours. Finally, she spoke.

"Sam is home, resting. His mom thinks it was a bear attack."

I couldn't even nod in acknowledgment. I hurt Sam.

"I know you think it was your fault, but it wasn't."

"How do you know?" My voice came out hoarser than I had ever heard it.

"Melissa said she saw a hooded figure retreating into the woods."

I looked at her. A hooded figure?

"That creature was after me."

"We think so," Aunt Jasmine said, a sad note to her voice.

I nodded weakly. A Jaramoth. A hooded figure. It was him, the witch who Richelle had been working for. He went after me, and Sam almost died because of it.

My face heated, and my chest constricted. How dare he mess with my friends? My family is one thing. They can handle themselves. But my friends were defenseless against this type of attack. My fists clenched and Aunt Jasmine immediately noticed the change. Her hand moved from mine to put it on my shoulder. Not as a sympathetic gesture, but as a warning for me to calm down. I was way past being calm, though.

Whoever this witch was, he was going down. I would make sure of it.

CHAPTER THIRTEEN

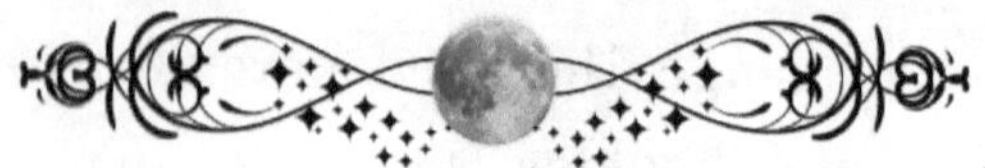

THAT EVENING, I WENT over to Sam's house to check on him. He had his blackout curtains down, even though it was already dark out. I dragged a chair over to his bed and sat down.

Sweat covered Sam's face and each breath he took sounded shaky. He shivered, and I pulled the covers over him. He noticed the extra weight and opened his eyes.

"Hey," I said.

"What do you want?" he replied weakly.

"I just wanted to check on you."

"Funny. You didn't want to check on me when I was getting mauled by a four eyed monster."

I flinched. He was right. I just stood there.

"I will make it right," I vowed.

He said nothing else as I sat there. Sam was mad at me, and rightly so. I stood up, kissed his forehead, and left without another word.

Instead of going home, I headed to the library. If anything was going to have the information I needed, it was bound to be the musty books in the back.

Someone whistled. I whirled around and groaned. Fabian approached me casually, grinning. I wanted to smack that grin off of his smug face.

"Hey there," he said.

"Go back to hell where you came from," I snapped.

"Well, that's not nice. Especially after your little boyfriend hit me with a tree limb."

"He's not my boyfriend."

"Can I be?"

I rolled my eyes and started to walk away. He caught up with me and matched my strides.

"Okay, wait," he said as he tugged me to a stop.

"What?" I demanded.

"I wanted to say I'm sorry. For—"

"For forcing yourself on me?" I finished for him.

He nodded. I scoffed and wiggled out of his grasp. My gut told me something about him was off, but I didn't know exactly what was wrong, so I ignored it.

"I'm not good at this. Please forgive me."

"Not good at what?" I asked, folding my arms against my chest.

"Being around a girl that... that I like this much."

"For future reference, if you like a girl, you probably don't want to force her to kiss you."

"I know. I—I'm sorry. Please. I'll do anything to make it up to you."

I pursed my lips as I weighed his words. He didn't seem like he was putting on an act. I huffed and lowered my arms.

"Fine. I forgive you."

His smile was immediate. I could see his eyes glowing with warmth. He rushed in and drew me into a hug. I stiffened. He backed off immediately and looked sheepish.

"Sorry," he said. "I didn't mean to do anything you didn't want to do. I just got carried away."

"A hug is fine." I smiled and bumped him lightly with my shoulder. "Just don't make a habit of it."

He stood at attention and nodded sternly. I laughed and he relaxed and laughed along with me.

I heard a rustling in the bush, and I stopped laughing immediately. I shushed Fabian and looked over to where the noise was coming from. My heart pounded in my chest as my body went on high alert. I wasn't making the same mistake twice. I grabbed a large stick and raked it through the leaves. When nothing moved or growled, I relaxed. I dropped the stick and went back to where Fabian was.

"What was that about?" he asked.

"Nothing," I said. He didn't need to be in danger as well.

He scrutinized my face. He could tell I was holding something back.

"You can tell me anything. Remember that, Ebony."

At that moment, I felt as if I could tell him anything. I wanted to tell him everything.

Something held me back, though. A little voice in my head said no, and for once I listened to it.

"Really, it's nothing. Sam got attacked by a bear earlier today, and I just wanted to make sure what I heard wasn't a bear."

"You were going to face a bear... with a stick?" he asked skeptically.

I shrugged. If only he knew bears were the safest thing in this town at the moment.

He laughed and rolled his eyes. "Only you could make that not sound bizarre."

"I am a not bizarre girl," I said.

"Of course you are. So can I walk the definitely not bizarre girl home?"

"I'm not going home. I'm actually going to the library."

"Can I come with you?"

"I'd rather go alone, to be honest."

"You just said there was a bear running loose, and that it attacked your friend, so I doubt it's friendly. Let me walk you," Fabian insisted.

I couldn't say no to his logic, so we walked the rest of the way together in a comfortable silence. When we got to the library, he seemed like he really wanted to come in with me, but I told him again I'd rather go alone. He nodded reluctantly and gave me one last hug goodbye. A smile grew on my face as I watched him walk away. Maybe he wasn't such a bad guy after all.

I made a beeline for the back and started looking through all the books, piling anything that I thought would be useful on a table. After I had looked through all the shelves twice, I began my reading.

I was there for several hours, and the words kept swimming off the page. I grabbed the book I was reading and threw it across the room in frustration.

"Did the book have it coming?"

I jumped and turned toward Aunt Jasmine, who was leaning against a shelf.

"What are you doing here?"

"I work here, smarty," she said.

"It's like midnight." I retrieved the book I had thrown.

"Actually, it's two fourteen, but who's keeping track?"

"Apparently you are."

She sat down next to me and picked up the book on top of my ever growing to-be-read pile.

"Getting anywhere?" she asked, flipping open the cover.

"No. Just a bunch of words that mean nothing," I said as I slammed the book back open to the page I left off on.

"Don't give up. We'll find out what's going on."

"It would help if I knew what I was looking for." I muttered.

Aunt Jasmine tugged on her ponytail. "It looks like you have all the right books, though. History of our realm, bestiaries, spell books. You're doing a good job."

"Then why haven't I found anything?" I snapped.

"Because I think you're right. We're missing something. Something big."

I nodded and turned back to reading. Aunt Jasmine flipped through a few pages until she found something curious, and we fell into silence.

"This is interesting," I said. The book I held was called *Hidden History of Amethystia* and I read what I found out loud.

"'The Amberwood family has ruled over the magical realm for three generations, but before the Amberwoods, the Delacroix family ruled for seven generations. Alaric Delacroix conceded power when Dante Amberwood beat him in a duel. Dante Amberwood banned dueling shortly after claiming the throne.'"

"That is interesting," she agreed. "I had heard about the Delacroix family, but only in passing. I never knew they ruled for that long." Aunt Jasmine's tone sounded off, but then again, it was almost three in the morning.

"Do you think they're trying to take us down?" I asked.

Aunt Jasmine shook her head. "Impossible. The family died out decades ago."

A knot formed in my stomach. Aunt Jasmine may have thought the family died out, but I had my doubts.

After a half hour of more research, Aunt Jasmine suggested we should get back to the house. I was too tired to read another word. We put the books back where we found them and went home.

Everyone was asleep, so we quietly went to our rooms. I checked the clock. Three forty-five in the morning and I had to be up for school in three hours. Groaning, I took off my shirt and tossed it on the bed. I was about to take my bra off when I caught a movement out of the corner of my eye. I whirled around and was about to scream when a hand clamped over my mouth.

A dark, hooded figure stood before me. My breathing hitched and my eyes widened. The hood didn't cover his face, and for good reason. He had no face. It was just a black swirling void. Nothing was there at all. But a noise came out of the void, like he was trying to calm me.

"Don't scream. It's alright," the disembodied voice said. "I'm going to uncover your mouth because I need some answers. But you're not going to scream, are you?"

I shook my head. This was giving me some serious déjà vu of when I snuck into Richelle's room and said almost the same thing to her.

The hooded figure released his hand. I straightened and peered into the faceless void with defiance. No way I was letting this creep get what he wanted.

"What did you find out tonight at the library?" he asked.

"Nothing."

"Don't lie to me," the voice said harshly. "What did you find out tonight at the library?"

"Nothing of interest."

Or did I find something of interest? The hooded figure obviously wouldn't have been here if I wasn't onto something. I needed to get back to the library.

The hooded figure's hand wrapped around my throat, cutting off my oxygen.

"I will ask you one more time. What. Did. You. Find?"

He tightened his grip with every word and by the time he finished asking, I was gasping for air.

"Nothing. I swear."

My door flung open before the hooded figure could snap my neck in two, and Nightshade came hurtling in. He tackled the hooded figure to the ground, and I bent over with my hand on my throat, coughing, trying to catch my breath and get the oxygen back to my brain.

The hooded figure recovered quickly and flew out the window. Literally. Nightshade cursed and quickly rushed to my side.

"Are you all right?" he asked.

All I could do was gasp and nod. Nightshade guided me to the bed and gently helped me sit down.

He sat beside me, stroking my back until my breathing was back to normal.

"I'm fine," I said hoarsely. "Did you see he had no face?"

"I saw. Are you sure you are okay?"

I tried to nod, but my neck hurt at the slightest movement. Nightshade noticed me wince, and he gently lifted my head to get a better look at my neck.

He sighed. "There will be some bruising. We are just lucky he did not crush your windpipe."

"He would have if you hadn't burst in when you did."

"I am glad I did. I could have lost you." Nightshade's face fell. "I feel like I already am."

"Why would you think that?" I asked.

Nightshade didn't answer. I put my hand under his chin and turned his head so he would look at me. He wouldn't meet my eyes.

"Nightshade, why would you think you're losing me?"

"I saw you. With him. You looked happy."

"With who?" It clicked right as I said it. The rustling in the bushes earlier wasn't a monster. It was Nightshade. Nightshade saw me joking around with Fabian.

"Oh Nightshade." I stroked his cheek. "Fabian is just some guy I go to school with. He's a jerk."

Nightshade looked me in the eye.

"So, you do not have feelings for him, then?" he asked.

I didn't want to tell Nightshade that I had a couple of hot and heavy make-out sessions with Fabian. At the same time though, I wanted to be honest with him. He deserved that.

"I... thought I had feelings for him. At one time."

"You thought you did? Would you explain that?"

It was my turn not to meet his eyes.

"Ebony, please tell me."

I took a deep breath and told him everything. When I looked at his face, I flinched. He didn't look angry. He looked hurt. Betrayed. My vision went blurry with tears as I tried to course correct. He brushed my hand away from his face and stood up.

"Was this before or after you confessed feelings for me?"

"Before. I swear," I pleaded.

The air felt like it was getting sucked out of the room as Nightshade left without another word.

CHAPTER FOURTEEN

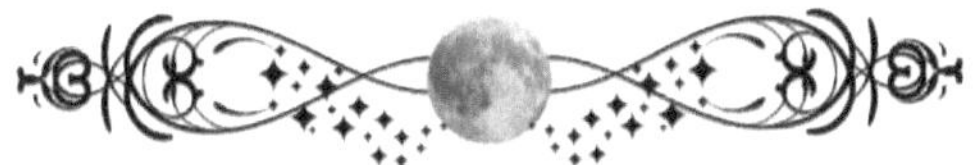

A N EARTHQUAKE JOLTED ME awake, then I realized it was just Aunt Jasmine shaking me from my sleep. I swatted her away and rolled over.

"Wake up! You're going to be late!" she shouted.

I groaned as I pulled the covers over my head. Aunt Jasmine sighed and whisked my warmth away. I curled up into a ball and squeezed my eyes shut.

"If you don't get up right now, I swear I will zap you out of that bed."

I glared at her through squinted eyes. "You wouldn't dare."

"Want to bet?"

I sprang out of bed and put my hands up in surrender. Aunt Jasmine smiled and walked out of the room. It was bad enough that I stayed up until four am, but nightmares riddled my mind with images of the black-bladed sword during the two hours of sleep I got. I looked in the mirror and sighed. The bruises on my neck were a startling black color. I gently probed the area, and winced. Whoever that hooded figure turned out to be, he was going to pay. I changed into a baby blue turtleneck sweater and checked the calendar. Eight days before the end of the world, and I was going to school.

Classes went by relatively quietly. Melissa only said a few words to me. Fabian smiled and waved. Uncle Hesperus wasn't in class, and I made a note to ask him about that later.

I was at my locker getting ready to head home when Fabian came up to me.

"Hey," he said.

"Hey."

"Your sweater looks good. I like that color on you." He looked me up and down, checking me out.

"Thanks." I muttered, finding the gesture slightly creepy.

"Can I walk you home?" he asked.

"I'm going to the library."

"I never pegged you for such an avid reader."

I shut my locker and smiled, ignoring the subtle dig.

"Walk me there."

As Fabian and I headed to the library, he told me all about where he lived before coming here. I had wondered, but I never voiced any questions. It would lead to a talk about where I grew up...

"Have you ever been?" Fabian asked.

I jolted my attention back to him and was unsure how to answer the question.

"Been where?" I asked.

"California. Where my parents raised me. Have you been paying attention?"

I pursed my lips, hoping I looked apologetic.

He rolled his eyes and smiled. "Of course not. Your head's somewhere else."

"Sorry."

Fabian shrugged. "No big deal. I know you're probably worried about Sam."

I nodded. It was weird, but when I was with Fabian, everything else seemed to just... melt away. When I was with him, I had no worries. I knew I should have been thinking about Sam and whether he was okay, but I just wasn't.

We arrived at the library, and I stopped short. Nightshade sat on a bench by the door, reading. He looked up and his face changed from neutral to downright hostile. He leaped up from the bench and marched toward us. I opened my mouth to say something. Anything. But he walked right past us and didn't once look back. A knot formed in my stomach as I watched his retreating figure. I had really hurt him.

Fabian shook my shoulder to get my attention, and I looked up at him. His face changed. He was no longer annoyed. His features softened and his thumb stroked my cheek, wiping away a tear.

"Who was that guy?" he asked.

"He's uh—he's my—I don't know what he is," I admitted.

Fabian stared at the ground and started shuffling his feet.

"Do you... like him?" Fabian asked hesitantly.

I nodded.

"Do you... like me?" he said in the same hesitant tone.

Did I like Fabian? He was hot, but no matter how hot he was, that didn't excuse his earlier behavior. Not to mention I had a gut feeling that something wasn't right, but I didn't want to hurt his feelings.

"I like you as a friend."

"Good. I like you too, only as more than a friend."

"I know," I said.

He kissed my cheek again and sauntered away. I stood where I was for a good five minutes, hating my life.

I was in the library for an hour before I couldn't take any more research. My eyes drooped, words melded together, and I had to reread the same paragraph at least five times. I shelved the books and wandered around the library, looking for Aunt Jasmine.

Instead, I found Melissa with the study materials. I walked up to her table and stood awkwardly, waiting for her to look up.

"What do you want?" she said without so much as a glance in my direction.

"Can I sit?"

She gestured to the empty chair across from her. I sat down and twiddled my thumbs, searching for the right thing to say.

"I want to—" I started.

"You just stood there." She glared daggers at me.

"I know."

"Sam got hurt, and you just stood there."

"I know. I—I'm sorry. I froze. I didn't know what to do."

"You get your head out of your ass, and you save your friend. *That's* what you do."

Melissa slammed her books shut and walked off. I exhaled. I would make it right.

My feet dragged on the ground by the time I opened the front door. I dropped my stuff down in the entryway and plopped down on the couch. I hauled a blanket over myself and waited for the sweet bliss of sleep to take me.

Of course, no such luck. The back door slammed open and in walked Aunt Jasmine and Uncle Hesperus, fighting yet again.

I groaned and pulled the blanket over my head. It did nothing. So, I groaned even louder, threw off the blanket, and walked into the kitchen to see what was going on.

"You can't leave right now!" Aunt Jasmine slammed her hand on the counter, making me jump.

"It's my duty! Something you wouldn't know about!" Uncle Hesperus pointed a finger directly in Aunt Jasmine's face.

"I wouldn't know about duty? You don't even know what I went through! My entire life, they taught me duty!" Aunt Jasmine threw her arms wide.

"And you threw it all away for the human realm!"

"I haven't seen you complaining much about this place these past few weeks!"

"Stop it!" I yelled.

They both looked at me, breathing hard.

"I'm so tired of you two fighting. Aunt Jasmine, I don't know what you went through, but get over it. And Uncle Hesperus, no one has been keeping you here except you. Go if you want, but leave me be so I can sleep!"

I stomped up to my room and slammed the door. I flung myself on my bed and my lips quaked. Tears welled up in my eyes as sobs took over my body.

I never cried that hard before. My whole body was shaking, my stopped up nose kept me from breathing, and my throat became sore.

I sobbed over Richelle, and how she'll never see graduation because of me. I sobbed over Sam, who was lying in bed, wrapped in bandages, and I was sobbing over me. Because I didn't know who I was anymore, and that scared me more than anything. The tears eventually slowed to a trickle, and then they stopped altogether.

I heard a knock on the door, followed by the turning of the knob. Someone sat down on the edge of bed and started stroking my hair.

"I'm so sorry, Ebony." Aunt Jasmine said, her touch calming me enough I could talk.

"S'okay." I managed between shallow breaths.

"Oh, you brave girl. It doesn't have to be okay all the time."

"Yes, it does."

Aunt Jasmine laughed without humor. "It's hard to remember sometimes you're still just a kid. You've grown up so much."

I sat up and faced her.

"I feel like I've grown down."

"Grown down?"

"Like I've regressed in maturity."

Aunt Jasmine wrapped her arms around me. "I feel that way too sometimes, but it's just a part of figuring out who you're truly meant to be."

I looked at her and saw nothing but love in her eyes. I gave her a big hug and told her I wanted to apologize to Uncle Hesperus.

"He's already gone," Aunt Jasmine said.

"He is?"

She nodded.

"What about my vision?"

"He's going to try to stop whoever is after us from home. There was... an urgent matter there he had to take care of."

"I saw him," I whispered.

"Saw who?"

"The hooded figure. The witch who's after us."

"When?" Aunt Jasmine asked, alarmed.

"Last night. He was here in my room. He would have killed me if Nightshade hadn't rescued me."

"He was in the house?" She stiffened.

I nodded. I pulled down the collar on my sweater and showed her the bruises.

Aunt Jasmine gasped as she lightly brushed her fingers across my neck.

"He had no face." I said.

"What do you mean 'no face'?"

"It was like a black hole. Cold. Dark. Empty."

"That's very dark, forbidden illusion magic." Aunt Jasmine said.

"Is it Soul Sorcery?"

Aunt jasmine shook her head. "Much darker. Soul Sorcery depends on your own life force to give spells power. This is called Necrotic Conjuring. I've only ever read about it. The magic works by killing someone and taking their life essence to fuel the spell. The first and only recorded use of it was from over two thousand years ago. A man had an affair with his wife's sister. His wife was so distraught and full of rage that she killed her sister and used Necrotic Conjuring to kill her husband. It was the rage of seeing them together that let her access that kind of magic in the first place."

We sat in silence after that. Whoever was after my family was killing people to get to us. They weren't just evil. They were insane. So how were we supposed to stop them?

I was walking along my usual path to school when someone grabbed me from behind. I screamed and wiggled out of their grasp.

"Gotcha!" Sam said, laughing.

"Sam!" I cried. I flung my arms around him and immediately let go for fear of hurting him. He must have noticed my expression. He twirled around, arms wide.

"I'm okay, Ebony. Not even a scar."

"How?"

"Nightshade healed me. He said it was his family's magic or something."

My smile turned into a look of confusion. "Why aren't you mad at me?"

He turned thoughtful. "I was. I should still be mad at you. With everything you went through with Richelle, though, it seemed like punishment enough."

"I'll be fine," I said with fake confidence.

"I know you will be. You just weren't then."

"Is Nightshade with you?" I asked.

"No. He said he was leaving today. Back to Amethystia."

My heart stopped. He was leaving? Without even saying goodbye?

"I have to go." I turned back toward the house.

My feet were in motion already, so I didn't hear what Sam called back. I willed myself to go faster. I wished I could fly. Or teleport. I reached the house in record time and flung open the door. I ran down the hall to Nightshade's room. The door was ajar, and I stopped just inside and looked around. His things were still there. I hadn't missed him. I put my hands on my knees and tried to catch my breath.

"Ebony?"

I whirled around and found Nightshade standing behind me.

"You can't leave," I said.

Nightshade's expression turned sad.

"I have asked to return home and continue my duties there. It is too hard being here. Seeing you with other boys hurts too much. I want to be with you Ebony, but you have made it perfectly clear you do not want to be with me."

"That's not true!" I cried.

"Is it not? Then tell me, why would you kiss that other boy when you supposedly had feelings for me?"

"It was before I knew I had feelings for you. I was upset and confused."

Nightshade raised an eyebrow. "Were you not upset and confused when you kissed me?"

"No. I kissed you because of what you make me feel."

"And how do I make you feel?" His face was neutral, but it looked like he was barely holding it together.

"You make me feel like the world isn't going to end. Like there is something left to live for.

Every time I'm around you, I get butterflies in my stomach and I can hardly speak. My body lights up when you touch me, and when you kiss me, I can't breathe. You make me feel alive. More alive than I've ever felt."

"It sounds like I should stop kissing you."

"I don't want you to."

"And that other boy? How does he make you feel?"

Nightshade's eyes were too vulnerable. I couldn't lie to him.

"He makes me feel enraged. But he also makes me feel like I have no responsibilities. Like I can just be a kid. He makes me feel free."

Nightshade nodded like he suspected as much.

"Please don't go," I said.

"I cannot stay," he said.

Tears fell down my cheeks freely as Nightshade moved past me and shut his door. I heard the lock click telling me I was not welcome.

I banged on the door, begging him to let me in. I banged until my hand hurt and I fell onto the floor, still banging, but I knew he wouldn't answer. Nightshade was gone.

CHAPTER FIFTEEN

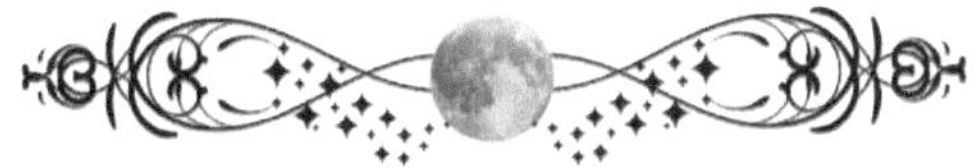

I DIDN'T KNOW HOW long I sat on the floor with my back to the cold wood, but after a while I got up and brushed away the last of the tears. If he wanted to leave, fine. I wouldn't waste my time pining over him. I had more important things to do.

I trudged to the kitchen and looked at the clock. Half-past eleven. He had been gone for a little over three hours. I felt my eyes getting wet again and closed them tightly. Taking a deep breath, I opened them. Do not pine. I made myself a sandwich, but all I did was pick at it, thinking about what Nightshade was doing. Was he helping Uncle Hesperus try to stop whatever was going down in just a little over a week? Or was he at home thinking about me like I was thinking about him? I pushed that thought out of my head because I didn't have time to sit and wallow when doomsday was right around the corner. I thought about the paragraph I had read in the library and how I couldn't shake the feeling that the sword and the Delacroix family were connected. Tossing what was left of my sandwich in the trash, I went to the entryway to grab my jacket. I was going to find out more about this family.

Walking to the library, I had plenty of time to think about Nightshade. I tried not to, but the look of absolute sorrow on his face haunted me. I had hurt him that badly by just kissing another guy. When we weren't even a thing yet. I picked up a stone from the road and screamed as I hurled it as far as I could throw.

"Ow!" someone yelled.

I looked over to where the voice came from and noticed Fabian rubbing his head.

"What are you doing here?" I asked.

"Getting stoned to death, apparently. Hitting me with a log wasn't good enough for you?"

"It wasn't a log, it was a very large stick. And I'm sorry, I wasn't aiming for you."

Fabian chuckled. "Got a bit of a temper, huh?"

I was always armed with sarcasm and wit, but not a temper. "No. Things have just been... hard these past few days."

"Want to talk about it?"

I shook my head.

"Okay," He said simply and started walking away.

"Hey!" I yelled, catching up to him. "What are you doing out of school?"

"I could ask you that same question." He said with a smirk. Our feet hitting the pavement sounded against the quiet street.

"I was at home." I said.

"Pathetic answer."

"Well, what were you doing?" I asked, crossing my arms.

"I was taking a walk, enjoying the nice fall air."

"Pathetic answer." I said.

"So, I guess we're both pathetic. Want to be pathetic together? We could go to the park."

"The last thing I want to do is go to the park with you. Last time wasn't so great, remember?"

He nodded and rubbed his head again. A chilly breeze blew by me and I shivered. Fabian took off his jacket and put it around my shoulders.

"Where are you headed?" Fabian asked, securing his jacket around me better as a gust of wind blew across us.

"The library," I said.

"And the book nerd strikes again."

"I'm not a book nerd. I just have a project I'm working on. "

"The library sounds great. I think I'll come with you. As long as we're both cutting class, that is."

What was I supposed to say to him? That I was going to do some magical research in the section of the library no one knew existed? He wouldn't believe that even if I told him. But I couldn't exactly tell him he couldn't come in with me because what if he does, anyway? I mean, it's a public place. I'd just have to ditch him when I was there.

We had barely been walking for five minutes, however, when a high-pitched shriek came from behind us. Fabian and I covered our ears tightly and sank to the ground from the pain. We turned around to see what had made the sound and my heart skipped a beat.

The ugliest creature I had ever seen stood about ten yards away. About four feet high and nearly as wide, it had stubby legs, and puke green skin, which was covered with oozing puss-filled pockets. Its nose was long and curved and jagged teeth stuck out of its mouth. Attached to its stubby arms were hands with only three fingers. In those hands, it held a wooden club almost as big as it was. I glanced at Fabian, who held a look of absolute horror. He didn't know what was going on and shouldn't have been here. He shouldn't have even been around me. Not when all this was happening.

The creature let out another shriek, and its yellow eyes locked on to me. It lumbered toward me faster than I thought its legs could carry it. Fabian grabbed my hand and pulled my attention away from the creature. We ran as fast as we could, but we only got about five yards when two more of those creatures barged out of the woods. We were surrounded.

My eyes darted between the creatures before my eyes caught Fabian's. His eyes were wide with terror. I had to protect him and I promised myself he wouldn't get hurt. I shouldn't have let Sam get hurt. My hand slipped out of Fabian's and I steadied my breathing. No one was going to like what I was about to do. I took a deep breath and thrust my hand toward the two creatures in front of us.

"*Electricae!*" I shouted.

A bolt of pure electricity shot out of my palm and fried both creatures in a second. I turned my attention to the creature behind us and thrust out my palm again, letting out another stream of electricity. The creature shrieked and dropped his club as he waddled away. My arm shook as I lowered it to my side. I had protected Fabian, and I didn't freeze up like I did the last time. I turned back to Fabian, who gaped at me as if I had grown another head.

I froze, careful not to make any sudden movements.

"Fabian?" I asked cautiously. "Are you okay? Did they hurt you?"

Fabian opened his mouth and closed it again. Taking a deep breath, I spoke again.

"I know what you saw must have scared you. I'm sorry."

Fabian nodded slightly.

"Can you say something?" I asked.

"Wh—What are you?"

"I'm a witch."

Fabian and I hurried the rest of the way to the library in an awkward silence. I didn't know what else to say to him, and he offered no more conversation.

We arrived at the front door of the library and just stood there like dorks.

"Let's go." He stepped forward, but I stopped him before he got too far.

"Wait. My aunt works here and—"

"Is she a witch too?" Fabian paled.

I nodded.

"Great." He trembled and I squeezed his hand in comfort.

"Well, I think it would be a good idea if she didn't know about us... almost dying, and me telling you about..."

I didn't think it would be this awkward. I thought it would have been nice to have Fabian know about me being a witch.

"Right," Fabian agreed.

We walked inside and I made a beeline for the back. Fabian followed me hesitantly. When we got to the space where the normal library ended and "construction" began, Fabian gave me a questioning look.

"It's okay. This part of the library is where we keep all our secret books on magic and stuff."

"And you're letting me see it?" His voice filled with excitement.

I nodded and grabbed his hand. The protection charms let him pass, and I led him straight to my table in the very back. I dropped his hand and gathered the books on the history of Amethystia. I sat them down on the table and Fabian gave them a wary look.

"Your project involves this many books?" he asked.

"Yeah. It's ridiculous."

He shrugged and sat down. I joined him, pulled the book I had been reading last out of the pile, and opened it.

I had been reading for less than five minutes when Fabian scooted his chair closer and leaned over my shoulder. I stiffened a little, but then relaxed as I told myself there was nothing to worry about.

"Anything interesting?" he asked.

"Why? Are you bored?" I asked with a tight smile.

"Out of my mind."

I giggled. I had to admit, as much as I hated reading, I loved learning about the history of home. It made me feel like I was back there, and I was learning a lot of things about my realm that I had never known.

I grabbed a book from the pile and handed it to Fabian. This one was about a record of people who had ruled the realm.

"Here. Why don't you help me research?"

"What am I looking for?" he asked, taking the book from me.

"Anything mentioning the Delacroix family. They were the ruling family of Amethystia before my family took over."

"Your family... rules your realm?"

I nodded sheepishly.

"Wow," he mouthed.

"Yeah. It's... not as fun as you might think."

"So, what's the deal with this other family?" He opened another book and started flipping through pages.

"It's complicated. Just look for anything mentioning them and I'll look at it."

"Got it."

We studied together like that for a while. Fabian would find a section mentioning the Delacroix family and I would read it to see if it was relevant. Nothing was. Defeat started to creep in when a book slammed on the table next to me and Fabian.

"Aunt Jasmine!" I yelped.

"Who's your friend Ebony?" she asked in a very disapproving tone.

With a glance at Fabian, I took a deep breath and recounted everything that had happened earlier as fast as I could.

"You were attacked? Again?" Her eyes widened and she plopped down in a chair, like her legs wouldn't hold her weight anymore.

"Yeah. Do you know what those things were? I have never seen them before."

Aunt Jasmine shook her head. I sighed. She was the only one I knew who was well versed in magical knowledge. Well, except for my dad, but I wasn't about to go there.

She sat across from Fabian and me, and grabbed a bestiary out of the pile of books I had yet to touch. She looked at us expectantly, and I understood she wanted us to get back to reading.

So we did just that. Aunt Jasmine, Fabian, and I looked through book after book until the sun went down. Still, none of us could find anything.

"I think we should call it a night," Aunt Jasmine said after she shut the third bestiary.

"I agree." Fabian yawned. "If I don't get home soon, the parents will flip."

Aunt Jasmine raised an eyebrow at Fabian but said nothing.

We were on our way home when she halted the car on the side of the road and looked at me with her mouth set in a thin line.

"I'm guessing I'm in trouble," I said.

She just continued to stare at me like that until she let out a sigh, and her face relaxed.

"How well do you know that boy?" she asked.

"Honestly? Not very well."

"So, you just told a human that you barely know the truth?" she asked incredulously.

"I told you, I didn't have a choice. Those things, whatever they were, attacked us."

"That's what bothers me. From what you told me, those creatures weren't attacking you. It sounded like they were herding you."

"Why?" I whispered.

"That's what I would like to know." She pulled back onto the road.

"So, you're not mad?" I asked.

"Oh, I'm mad," she said, staring at the road. "Just be glad your uncle isn't here anymore. He'd be furious."

I stared at the trees going by, thinking about what Uncle Hesperus would have done if he were here. Probably kill Fabian. Then me. Or maybe the other way around.

Aunt Jasmine pulled into the driveway and stopped the car. I noticed lights were on inside the house.

"Did you leave the lights on?" Aunt Jasmine grabbed my shoulder.

I shook my head.

"Stay here." She got out of the car and quietly shut the door. She dramatically snuck to the front door as she took off her purse, readied it as a weapon, and burst into the house.

A few minutes later, she sticks her head out the front door and motions for me to come in. I undo my seatbelt and get out, closing the door normally. I head to the living room and stop dead in my tracks. Sitting on the couch across from Aunt Jasmine were my parents.

CHAPTER SIXTEEN

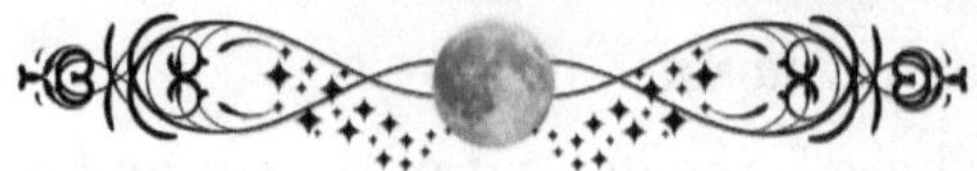

I SAT IN A chair across from my parents in the living room while Aunt Jasmine fixed tea. My leg bounced up and down with nervous energy and my fingers twiddled as I tried not to think about why they were here.

"Quit fidgeting Ebony." My mother sat upright in her chair, with her hands in her lap.

"I can't."

"Are you under a fidgeting curse?" My father stood at my mothers side, still as a statue.

"No, but I—"

"Then do as your mother says."

I sighed and tried to think of anything else except my rapid breathing and sweaty palms. My mother's hair. Brown except for a golden blonde strand she always kept braided. My dad's neatly trimmed beard. My mind kept wandering back to the day I got banished, though, no matter how hard I tried to erase it from my mind. I would always see the disappointment in my mother's eyes and the pure shame in my father's.

Aunt Jasmine came out of the kitchen a few minutes later, and I relaxed for real. She set teacups in front of everyone and sat in the chair beside me. She gave me an encouraging smile and turned to my parents.

"Luna, Horus. What brings you to the human realm?"

"We heard our daughter was causing trouble." Dad said.

"I see you talked to Hesperus." Aunt Jasmine sipped her tea.

"Yes. My brother told us all about what's going to transpire, and how our daughter seems to be in the middle of it all." My dad rigidly sat down and grabbed his teacup.

"That's not her fault," Aunt Jasmine said.

"I beg to differ," Dad said tightly.

"You always like to think the worst of me." I whispered, my head hung low.

"You've given me no other way to think." He took a sip of tea.

I swallowed back tears. Aunt Jasmine put her hand on my knee, comforting me.

"Ebony has been doing the best she can under the circumstances." Aunt Jasmine said.

"We don't doubt it," Mom said. "But we're afraid her best is not enough in this situation."

"Luna, you are my sister and I love you, but you don't know what's been going on with her lately."

"I know. Horus and I have been talking, and we think the best solution for everyone is if we take our daughter home," Mom put her hand on top of Dad's.

"What? No!" I sat up straight.

Aunt Jasmine's hand tightened on my knee. A warning.

"Hesperus banished her here to discipline her. Only he would have the power to rescind that punishment."

"I have talked to my brother. He agrees she should be at home with us, where we can monitor her," Dad said.

"And why didn't he mention that to me before he left?" Aunt Jasmine asked tightly.

"Probably because he didn't want to argue with you," Mom said.

"You can't take me back. I like it here. I like my friends and I enjoy watching movies and eating popcorn and having painting nights with Aunt Jasmine."

"What have you been filling her head with?" Dad asked Aunt Jasmine.

"She came here angry and broken. I gave her a safe space to express herself and heal," Aunt Jasmine said.

"Had it not been for that boy she was with, she wouldn't have needed to come here." Dad sat his teacup down sharply, making it clatter.

I tried to ignore the pain I felt when my dad mentioned my ex. I had done a good job of putting him out of mind. My head was hurting from all the arguing. I tried to ignore it.

"Jasmine, I'm sure you thought you were doing the right thing, but she is not your daughter. We agreed to send her to you for discipline, not play dates."

The headache got worse, and spots started covering my vision. Not again. I clutched my hands to the sides of my head and applied pressure, trying to ease some of the pain. The spots danced around my vision. People were saying things to me, but I couldn't hear them. They were miles away.

I stood on the bank on the White Run River, looking up at the sky. The enormous moon glowed blue. Halloween night. The sound of the river rushed by and the breeze was cold and uninviting. I looked around frantically.

People shouted as a hole ripped open in the bloodred sky. Flying creatures descended on the realm. I saw a movement on top of a crumbling ruin. The hooded figure had his hands raised toward the sky in triumph. A sword made of glowing metal glinted in one hand.

I felt a weird pull in the pit of my stomach, like the sword was calling to me. Everything else seemed to disappear. I rushed to the ruins, pushing my way through the people running all around me. Giant creatures swooped down, killing everyone they came in contact with.

Still, I ran.

I got to the ruins and the hooded figure was no longer on the top of them. He was right in front of me. Just like I remembered him, the faceless void looked into my soul.

He raised the black blade of the sword above his head and swung down.

I screamed as I came back to reality. Aunt Jasmine and my parents surrounded me, trying to get my attention. I gasped for air as I waved them off. They stepped back to give me some space. I was back home. Safe. I used that knowledge to calm my breathing.

"You had a vision." Aunt Jasmine put her hand on my shoulder, her face scrunched in concern.

"It was more vivid than the other times."

"What vision?" Dad asked.

"She's had visions of what's going to happen on Halloween." Aunt Jasmine said.

"Hesperus never told us that." Dad crossed his arms.

"He probably didn't want to you to worry."

"My daughter is having visions, and no one told us?"

"Dad, please stop." I put my hand to my forehead, now slick with sweat.

"Jasmine, I want to know what's going on. Now."

"Let's make sure Ebony is okay first, shall we?" Aunt Jasmine said.

My dad reluctantly agreed. Aunt Jasmine sent him to the bathroom to get a cold washcloth. Mom went to the kitchen to brew a potion for calming nerves, and Aunt Jasmine sat down beside me.

"I'm okay," I said.

"Sure. And I'm Cleopatra,"

I laughed once. "I'm not sure Cleopatra was a talented painter."

"I'm not sure she was either." Aunt Jasmine smiled halfheartedly.

Dad came back in the room and laid the washcloth over my forehead. He sat down on the couch, looking genuinely frightened.

"I'm okay, Dad," I said.

"I know. I've just... never seen you like that. Never seen you in that much pain. Even when you were in bed for a week, sick as a dog."

"I didn't mean to scare you all." I didn't think they would be this worried about me, and it made me bitter that they cared now.

Mom came back into the room a couple of minutes later and handed me a cup full of swirling herbs. It smelled like chamomile and lavender. I took a sip and my body instantly relaxed.

"What happened in your vision?" Mom knelt in front of me and laid a hand on my knee in comfort.

I recounted the vision to them as I sipped on the potion and dad interrupted me when I talked about the sword.

"What did it look like?" he asked.

I described every detail I could remember. Dad nodded and asked if there were any symbols on the sword.

"Yeah actually. It looked a lot like words to a spell."

Dad stroked his beard and turned thoughtful. I wanted to ask him what was so important about the sword, but I ended up yawning instead.

"You should get some sleep," Aunt Jasmine said, taking the cup from me so I didn't spill it all over the floor.

Mom helped me to my room. I dressed in pj's while she turned down the covers. She tucked me in and sat on the edge of the bed, and grabbed my hand.

"You should have told us sooner about the visions," Mom whispered.

"I know. I just couldn't."

"Do you hate us that much?" she asked, her voice somber.

"I don't hate you. I thought you hated me."

"Why would we ever hate you? You're our daughter." She tucked a strand of hair behind my ear with her free hand.

I smiled slightly as my eyes closed. Mom started humming a tune, and my eyes popped open.

"Do you not want me to sing you to sleep?" she asked.

"No, that's not it. I just haven't heard that song since I was little."

"I used to sing it to you all the time. You couldn't get enough of the tune." She started humming again and her eyes grew distant.

I smiled and closed my eyes again and I fell asleep to the sound of a lullaby from a lifetime ago.

I didn't want to wake up. The echo of Mom's lullaby rang in my head as I slowly opened my eyes. Clouds hung low in the sky and the streets were wet, like it had just rained. I stretched and got out of bed. I heard my parents talking to Aunt Jasmine as I headed downstairs. It made me feel weird, knowing they were here.

I walked into the kitchen, and all the talking stopped. I warily got a cup out of the cabinet and poured myself some coffee.

"What's going on?" I asked as I slowly sipped from the cup.

"Your parents are going to take you home today," Aunt Jasmine said.

"No! I thought we discussed this already."

"After that stunt you pulled last night, we decided without you." Dad clenched his jaw.

"Stunt?" I said, my vision turning red. "You think my vision was a stunt?"

"What your father meant to say was that it would be safer for you at home. Especially with your visions." Mom held her hands up as if confronting a cornered animal.

"Right." I rolled my eyes.

It wasn't fair. They thought I made it all up. Slamming my cup down on the counter, I went back to my room and quickly changed into a sweater and jeans. I ran downstairs and grabbed my jacket from the entryway, and slammed the front door on my way out. I jogged all the way to Melissa's house. She was probably getting ready for school, but I needed to talk to her.

I knocked on the door, and her father answered. He said Melissa was up in her room and that Sam was there, too. After thanking him, I walked through the house. I didn't even knock on Melissa's door as I walked in.

They looked at me in surprise. Before they could ask what was going on, I ran to them and wrapped them in a hug.

Melissa was the one to break the embrace.

"What happened to your neck?" she asked.

My hand immediately went to my throat. I had forgotten to wear anything to cover where the hooded figure strangled me, so my bruises were on full display. I vaguely wondered what Melissa's dad must have thought.

I sat down on Melissa's bed and filled them in on everything that had happened from that night to this morning.

"They can't take you home, can they?" Sam's eyes widened.

"They can, and they're going to."

"It's not right. You belong here. With us," Melissa said sadly as she sat beside me.

"I know, but they have their minds made up." I lowered my shoulders.

There was no way my parents were going to let me stay in the human realm. Especially after seeing my vision last night.

"We're coming with you." Sam had his chin set in a determined fashion. I had seen that face enough to know there was no changing his mind, but my parents would never agree to it, not to mention everyone else in the realm.

"You can't. No human has ever gone to Amethystia. Ever," I told them.

"We'll be the first ones." Melissa jumped up and paced the room. "We are not letting you go that easily. You are our friend, and if what you say is true, both worlds will be in ruins soon, so why not have a little fun before then?"

"You don't get it, guys," I explained. "My dad is an advisor to my uncle. The ruler of the entire realm. The king. He wouldn't break a rule like that."

"Then we won't tell him." Sam had a wicked gleam in his eye.

"How do you propose we sneak you guys into Amethystia? To get there, a portal has to be opened and I don't know how to open one yet," I said.

"Then we'll have to persuade your parents," Melissa said. "And I think I know how to do it. Forewarning, it's a bad plan."

I grinned, and the three of us put the plot in motion.

I walked into the house and found my parents sitting where I had left them in the kitchen.

"I'll go back on one condition," I said, my lips set in a thin line.

"And what condition is that, Ebony?" my mother asked in a bored manner.

"My two best friends come with me. Agree and I'll go without another word. Disagree and not only will I not go, I'll show my magic to the entire town."

"Don't be stupid, Ebony. Your friends are human. They can't come with us. Besides, I'm calling your bluff. Showing your magic to the human world wouldn't only expose you, it would expose your aunt as well." My dad tapped his foot on the wood floor, and crossed his arms.

"Sam and Melissa are outside with a video of me using my magic and they're ready to send it to the entire town of Salem. Of course, with the Internet, you can never be too sure if that video will stay in town," I tapped my lip with my finger.

Dad raised an eyebrow and set his mouth in a thin line. Mom gaped at me, appalled. Just like old times then.

"Are you insane?" Mom screeched.

"Just desperate," I said.

Dad took a deep breath and pinched the bridge of his nose.

"Jasmine!" Dad yelled.

Aunt Jasmine walked into the kitchen almost immediately. I bet she had heard everything.

"Yes?" she said with an innocent expression. I was right. She heard.

"Not only did you let my daughter tell *humans* about us, but you also let her get away with such egregious actions."

"I did not *let* her tell anyone. She did that on her own. And while I don't agree with how she's going about this, I agree that Sam and Melissa have earned the right to go with her. They need each other," Aunt Jasmine said calmly.

"I guess I have no choice." Dad sighed, shaking his head.

"Swear," I said.

"What?"

"Swear they can come with me."

Dad huffed and sagged his shoulders. "Fine. I swear by the light of magic, your friends can come to Amethystia with you."

I rushed outside to get my friends. When all three of us entered the kitchen, Dad looked at Sam and Melissa like he wanted to murder them.

"Delete the video. Now," he ordered.

"What video?" Sam asked with a sly grin.

"Oh, he means the video of Ebony using magic that never existed," Melissa said in an exaggerated tone.

Dad's face reddened and he narrowed his eyes.

"It wasn't their idea," I blurted, ashamed that I tricked my parents like that, but glad our plan worked. "It was mine. We bluffed. Sorry."

"Ebony Amberwood, so help me I will—"

"Abide by your word," my mother finished for him, taking a deep calming breath.

Dad was breathing hard, and he looked like he wanted to banish me to somewhere far worse than the human realm, but he looked at my mom and nodded once.

Sam, Melissa, and I excused ourselves and went up to my room to pack my things.

"That went well." Sam threw his arms up in elation.

"Better than I thought it would go." I started packing my clothes.

Someone knocked on the door a second before entering, and Aunt Jasmine looked at all three of us sternly.

"I'm sorry," I said.

"You should be."

"I didn't know what else to do. How else were they supposed to listen to me?" I pleaded.

"By talking to them, not threatening them," she said.

"I'm sorry," I said again. Sam and Melissa huddled in the corner, trying to pretend they didn't exist.

Aunt Jasmine huffed and sat on the bed. "I know you think you can't talk to them, but they're your parents. Try to open up to them once in a while. They'll listen."

"You weren't there," I said.

"Wasn't there when? Just now?" she asked.

I shook my head. "The day I got banished here. You didn't see the way they looked at me. The way they treated me. It was like I wasn't their daughter. Just some common criminal."

"Oh, Ebony." Aunt Jasmine put a hand on my shoulder. "I'm sure they were just angry. They would never cast you away like that."

"But they did! They cast me here without a second thought, and now they want to take me back just like that."

"I understand you're still hurt. I would be too, but they love you, no matter what you've done."

A single tear ran down my cheek. She was wrong. They never loved me. They just wanted a perfect little daughter to complete their happy little family.

Melissa wrapped her arms around my shoulders and squeezed. I smiled at her, but it didn't reach my eyes.

Mom came into the room just then. Melissa pulled away, and I waited for the eruption. It never came.

"It's time to go," Mom said, and then simply walked away.

CHAPTER SEVENTEEN

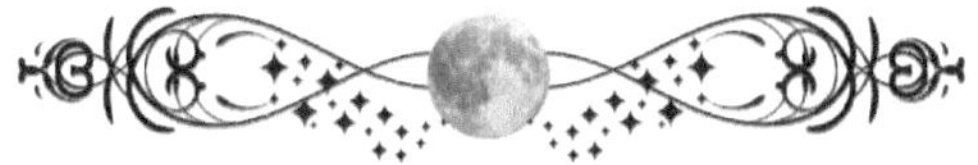

THE PORTAL TO AMETHYSTIA dropped us into the heart of my family's castle. Sam and Melissa were the last ones through and I could practically hear their jaws hit the floor. I watched them take it all in, and my chin lifted with pride. Even to me, the architecture of the castle was amazing. The thick cobblestone walls rose higher than any skyscraper, and purple ivy grew along the sides, inside and out. Hundreds of candles littered my uncle's throne room and illuminated the entire area like an ethereal dream.

The servants escorted Sam and Melissa to my wing and I followed. Their reactions were priceless when they saw my room.

"You like?" I asked with a laugh.

"We love!" Melissa squealed. She raced toward the oversized king bed and flung herself on it, making a Melissa sized dent in the bedding. Sam set his stuff down on my lounger and took in the entire room. The crystal chandelier in the middle spun, and rainbows danced over everything.

I gave them the grand tour and had to keep myself from laughing several times. Sam was in awe of the library, with its magnificent bookcases and floor-to-ceiling windows looking out to the terrace. Melissa absolutely loved the warm tones of the great hall and the smell of the cooking roast. I took them down to the servants' quarters and introduced them to everyone. The servants shot wary looks at them, but none spoke a word.

I guided them to my favorite spot in the castle last. The garden was underground, but flowers in every color imaginable bloomed brightly and the ceiling was littered with crystals, making the entire space seem like it was underneath the stars. An enormous pool in the middle of the garden reflected the light above. I guided them down the path and we dangled our feet in the crystal clear water.

"This place is amazing." Sam kicked his feet in the pool, making the reflections shimmer.

"I can't believe you live here." Melissa picked an aspedil, a light orange flower with royal blue coloring in the middle.

"It's a little bigger than Aunt Jasmine's house, isn't it?" I asked.

They both nodded as Melissa sniffed the aspedil, and Sam gazed at the ceiling.

I sighed. "I just wish my parents hadn't dragged her here, too."

"Why not?" Sam asked.

"Aunt Jasmine has a not so pleasant history with this place. I don't know the specifics of it, but she had to beg my uncle to let her leave the first time."

"And now?" Melissa asked.

I shrugged. Truthfully, I didn't know if Uncle Hesperus would let her leave again. I didn't know if he would let *me* leave again. The thought of never seeing the human realm again made me sad.

Ripples on the pool made the reflected lights dance. "I come here when I want to be alone." I said.

"Is that often?" Sam asked.

My eyes unfocused, and I nodded.

"I'm sorry." He looked down.

"It's okay. I've never had any friends I could talk to here. Everyone was either afraid of me or wanted something from my family."

"That seems... lonely," Melissa said.

"It was." I looked up at them and smiled. "But I have you two here now, so it won't be as lonely. At least not for a while."

"Right," they agreed.

The lunch bell echoed through the garden chamber, and I explained to Sam and Melissa what it meant. We dried our feet and put our shoes back on. When we arrived at the dining hall, I was surprised to see so many people.

The entire court sat around vast tables, drinking and laughing. They paused when we entered. Me, an outcast in my home, and my two human friends. Whispers started. Quiet at first, but they grew louder as I led Sam and Melissa to the table where we would be eating.

"The humans eat outside," one nobleman said, blocking our path before we could sit down.

"They will not," I said.

"You may be of the royal family, but I am the advisor—"

"You're the advisor to the advisor's advisor." I waved my hand dismissively. "Now move aside."

He huffed, but he did as he was told. I shot Sam and Melissa an apologetic glance and we sat down, Sam on one side of me and Melissa on the other. The servants brought our food out and we started eating.

"This is amazing!" Sam cried as he bit into the roasted leg of a Phaku Beast. People from every table watched with judgmental stares as my friends and I laughed and enjoyed ourselves.

After lunch, my uncle summoned us to the library where he and my father waited.

"Welcome home, Ebony," Uncle Hesperus said. "And welcome to Amethystia, Sam and Melissa."

"Thanks," I said. "What's with the summons? I was going to take Sam and Melissa on a tour of the town."

"That will have to wait," Dad said. "We have more pressing issues to attend to."

"Like what?" I asked.

Uncle Hesperus handed me a book opened to a picture of the sword I saw in my vision. I gasped.

"You recognize it?" Uncle Hesperus asked.

I nodded and handed the book back to Uncle Hesperus. He shut the book and put it back on the shelf.

"I knew it," Dad muttered and glanced at Uncle Hesperus.

"Knew what?" I asked.

"This is the sword of the Delacroix family. Each ruler passed it down to their successor." Uncle Hesperus bit his lip and his brow wrinkled. "We thought it was lost generations ago, but if you've seen it in one of your visions, as your father told me you have, then we have a big problem."

"How big of a problem?" I asked.

"The sword can open a portal to a hell dimmension, unleashing great monsters on both realms."

An ominous silence fell, and I broke it. "Oh, so huge trouble."

"We need to find that sword." Dad said.

"How do we find it if it's been lost for so long?" I asked.

"The Regelves should be able to guide you."

"That's Nightshade's race," I said.

"Yes, and speaking of..." Uncle Hesperus said as the door to the library opened. "Nightshade will accompany you on this journey."

I turned around. Nightshade stood in the doorway, staring at me. I looked for any sign that he might be happy to see me, but his expression remained impassive. My chest constricted. I couldn't breathe. It felt like forever since I had seen him, but it was only yesterday.

"We should get going," Nightshade said and walked out of the library.

Sam, Melissa, and I followed him. I had never seen where Nightshade lived before, but I was curious to find out.

Nightshade's people lived farther east than I would have expected. We trekked for about two hours in the wilderness until I saw smoke billowing up from a chimney.

Nightshade warned us that his people were wary of outsiders, human or not. He told us to wait by some boulders until he had talked to the village leader. He gave us the all clear soon after and we entered the quaint village.

Regelves went about their business shopping and making tools. Children played in the streets. Everyone gave us untrusting looks as we walked by, but when they noticed Nightshade, their fears seemed to ease a little.

Nightshade led us to the largest house in the village, though it was smaller than Aunt Jasmine's house. He opened the door for us and we filed in.

A fireplace burned in the corner hearth, casting everything with a warm glow, and a small wooden table smooth with years of use was set for five. Nightshade sat and the three of us followed suit.

He poured us drinks from the plain ceramic pitcher that was in the middle of the table. There was clinking in the other room, and a middle-aged lady with white hair down to her waist came out with a tray of goodies. She set them on the table and sat at the end. She must have been the village leader.

"I am Tirina. Nightshade tells me you are looking for the Delacroix family sword." She passed around a plate of fruits and bread. Sam, Melissa, and I all took some while Nightshade passed on the food.

"Yes ma'am, we are," I said.

"I might be able to help. My family served the Delacroix family for a long time. I believe it was five generations or so."

"So the sword is real?" I took a bite of an apple.

"Oh, it is very real, my dear. And very dangerous. Before I help you, I must ask, what do you want with the sword?" Her eyes scrutinized me and made me feel like I was under a microscope.

I looked at Sam and Melissa who were too busy eating to give me any guidance on what to say.

"I think the sword will help protect us all from the destruction that's coming."

"You mean the destruction of both realms that your visions have shown? My son has mentioned that."

"Nightshade is your son?" I asked curiously.

"Stay on task." Nightshade crossed his arms.

"Do not be rude, Nightshade," she said. "Yes. Nightshade is my son, and I am very proud he could serve your family. For however short a time it was."

"Short? He's still Ebony's bodyguard, isn't he?" Melissa asked.

"He has not told you all? Nightshade will leave the Amberwood's service after all this mess on Halloween is over."

Nightshade was leaving? Why? Did I hurt him that much?

His shoulders sagged. "Do not tell her anything else, Mother. I beg of you."

"Anyway, people say someone in the family buried the sword deep in an underwater cavern off the coast near the family castle. Many have searched, only a couple have come back. Empty-handed at that," she said.

I tried to focus on the task at hand and not on Nightshade, but every breath he took drew my attention to him. His face stayed neutral like back at Aunt Jasmine's house, but his emotions were starting to surface, and I wanted to reach out and touch him.

"Where's the castle located?" Sam asked.

"About a half a day south from here," she said.

"Then we better get going. Nightshade, can I talk to you?" I got up and made my way outside.

Nightshade gave his mother an exasperated look, but followed.

"You didn't tell me you were leaving the guard, too," I said as soon as the door shut behind him.

We stood so close together I could smell the vanilla and musk on him. It made it hard to concentrate, but if I affected him back he didn't show it.

"Why did I need to tell you that?" He asked.

"So I can stop you."

"Ebony, you cannot stop me from going. It is what is best for me. I cannot be around you anymore. I have to go." His eyes betrayed some of the emotion he was feeling. They were filled with hurt.

"No. You are not going anywhere. You're staying here. With me." Tears welled up in my eyes.

"Why should I stay?" he asked solemnly.

Instead of giving him an answer, I grabbed his face in my hands and kissed him. He grabbed my arms. I thought he was going to push me away, but he wrapped my arms around his neck, deepening the kiss. I moaned as his hands traced down my body, wrapping around my waist.

"Oh, my god," Melissa squealed.

We broke the kiss quickly. Nightshade's skin turned dark. He was blushing and so was I. Melissa whirled and went back inside with a giggle.

"We should probably follow her," Nightshade said.

"Are you staying?" I asked.

Nightshade pulled me in close, wrapping his arms around me, and kissed my forehead.

"I will stay," he answered simply.

I sighed and leaned into him. We broke the embrace and followed Melissa back inside the house.

Nightshade's mother gave me a knowing look as we both sat back down and my face caught fire.

"Tirina was just telling us about the path to the castle. She said it's been riddled with monsters for years." Sam's face held a hint of fear, but he was trying to be brave.

"And bandits," Melissa added, her face going white.

"We will go under cover of night then," Nightshade said. "Mother, may we stay here and rest until the sun goes down?"

"Of course, my son," she said. "I will get you supplies for your trip." She left the four of us alone at the table.

"There are spare rooms in the back," Nightshade said. "We all should get some sleep before we head out."

"Too bad there's no one to cuddle with here," Melissa said pointedly. My face reddened once more.

"I'll cuddle with you," Sam said, completely missing the pointed statement. "That is... if you want."

Now it was Melissa's turn to blush. I bit back a giggle. Melissa gave me a death glare and I shut up.

"That's very sweet, Sam, but I think I'm just going to go lie down. Alone." Melissa excused herself and went to the back of the house. I motioned Sam should follow her. He vehemently shook his head.

"You should get some rest, too," Nightshade said to me. "We have a big journey ahead of us."

As I got up, I nodded. I grabbed Sam by the collar and hauled him to the back of the house. I shoved him into the room that Melissa went into and I took the room directly across from it.

About five minutes later, I heard a knock. I answered it to find Nightshade on the other side, shifting his weight from one side to the other, and tugging at his clothes.

"Need something?" I asked curiously.

"Would you like me to—if you want I can—" His face blushed a deep scarlet, and I giggled as I took his hand and pulled him into the room.

"I would love it if you would cuddle with me." I said.

He smiled, and I got back into bed. I rested my head on his chest as he slid in beside me. He pulled the covers over us and laid his hand on my back, making soothing motions. We stayed like that until I fell asleep.

CHAPTER EIGHTEEN

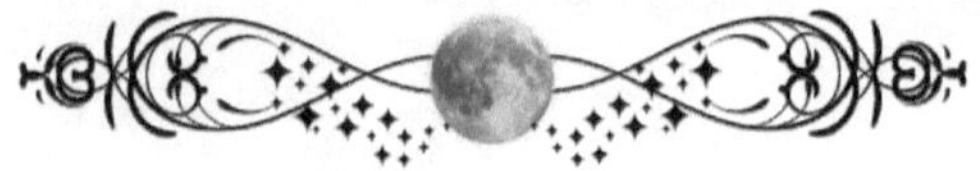

NIGHTSHADE WOKE ME A few hours later. The sun was setting, and we had to go. His mother packed each of us a knapsack full of food and first aid supplies, and she gave Nightshade a map of the area. We graciously thanked her and were off. The trek started off nice enough with the sky glowing a warm orange.

Things took a turn for the worse once the sun disappeared completely. The trees all looked the same. Nightshade swore up and down he was reading the map correctly, but the third pass by the same bush gave him pause. Sam and Melissa looked dead tired from all the walking, so we rested for a bit and took in our surroundings. I grabbed the map from Nightshade and looked at it myself.

"No wonder we're going in circles!" I cried. "The map is wrong!"

"Wrong?" Nightshade asked, looking over my shoulder. The heady smell of vanilla and musk filled my nostrils. "No, I am sure my mother gave us the correct map."

I nodded. "She gave us the right map, but see these trees?" I pointed to a spot on the map with a cluster of evergreens. "They aren't anywhere we've been. And these right here"— I pointed to a series of symbols framing the map— "these are words. They're just jumbled. I think this map is a riddle."

"Why would my mother give us a riddle?" Nightshade asked.

"To make sure we were worthy of getting the sword?"

"If it's a riddle, how do we solve it?" Melissa asked.

"Easy. We need a key," Sam said.

"A key? To what?" Nightshade asked.

"The words have been mixed around, right? Like a code." Sam started talking really fast and animatedly. "Well, we need a key to decipher them. A word or phrase that tells us how to read the map."

He asked for the map and I handed it over. It surprised me Sam liked riddles. On second thought, maybe it didn't because he tutored Melissa and me all the time. Sam surveyed it for a while before laying it out flat and pointing to the strange clump of evergreen trees.

"Those mysterious trees you mentioned? That's the only place on the map that seems to stand out. I think we'll find the key there." Sam's body bobbed up and down.

Melissa dug in our packs, pulled out some dried jerky, and passed it around to everyone while we planned. After we ironed out the details, we set out to find the cluster of pine trees.

Nightshade and I took turns examining the map and, after a few minutes of heated discussion, determined the way to go was northwest. About an hour into our journey, the scent of roasting meat led us to a group of bandits. Melissa's face turned green at the sight of rabbits roasting on a spit, and my stomach conveyed the same feeling.

Nightshade motioned us over to a thicket of trees where we would be hidden from sight.

"We need to get out of here," Nightshade whispered.

"How? There have to be at least forty of them." Melissa's eyes were wide and she clenched and unclenched her fists.

"There's actually five," Sam deadpanned.

"Well, that's still a lot!"

While they were arguing about how best to get around the bandits, I had come up with another idea. I stood up straight and marched directly into the bandit's camp.

Five swords turned on me and I took a deep breath, letting the earthy smell of the woods calm my nerves.

"Hey, guys," I said in a cool tone. "Got room for a few more outlaws?"

One man sauntered toward me. I assumed he was the leader by the way everyone was gauging his reaction to a teenage girl waltzing into their territory. The guy was big and burly, with deep brown skin and a crisscross scar running down the front of his face. His black hair was tied back into a ponytail and his deep green eyes assessed every move I made.

"What business do you have here, girl?" he asked in a voice that sounded higher than I expected.

"I was wondering if you could help my friends and me. See, we sort of stole something from the palace and now we're on the run from the *mighty* king." I said the last part with sarcastic emphasis, hoping they hated my uncle enough to give me what I wanted.

The big burly man laughed. "So, what did you steal? And where are these 'friends' of yours?"

I motioned to the trees where Sam, Melissa, and Nightshade still hid. They emerged one at a time. Nightshade first, disapproval written all over his face. Melissa next, and Sam pulled up the rear.

The burly man laughed even harder. "Hesperus Amberwood let a Regelf steal from him?" The entire group laughed with him.

Nightshade reluctantly handed over the map, and the burly man snatched it out of his hands.

"Well," he said, "I have to say, you all got guts. You risked your necks for a—looks like a treasure map." He handed the map back to Nightshade. "X marks the spot, eh, boys?"

The group of bandits busted out in laughter, the sound echoing through the forest. We weren't going to get anywhere if I didn't sweeten the lie.

"I stole it directly from the king's brother."

The laughter stopped dead. The burly man raised an eyebrow. Got him.

"Now, how did a small girl like you manage to do that?"

"Because I'm his daughter."

"Ebony," Nightshade said in warning. He put one hand on my shoulder and his other hand tightened on the grip of his sword.

"You're Ebony Amberwood? The exiled princess who used Soul Sorcery to defeat some kid in a duel?"

I nodded once.

The burly man whistled low. "And here I thought I was a badass. Name's Warwick. Take a seat and show me that map again."

We sat around the fire and two of Warwick's men were trying to figure out where the patch of evergreen trees was relative to our position

"It's gotta be north," one man with a glass eye said.

"No, it's the other way! South!" said another man through his three missing teeth.

"You're both idiots." Warwick said, snatching the map out of their hands and handing it back to me. "The trees on the map are due east, and it's called the Glade of the Hanged Man."

"You've been there?" I asked.

"Not personally, but I've been told stories by beautiful... people."

"He means to say beautiful women," one of the other men said. This one had a big brass ring hanging from his ear.

"Shut up!" Warwick ordered.

Earring guy shut his mouth with an audible snap.

I handed the map to Nightshade and stood up. "How far is the glade from here?"

Warwick rubbed his chin. "I don't know. Like I said, I've never been. But the stories say the glade will show itself only when it wants to, so you may get lucky and find it. Or not."

"Thanks for your help." I held out my hand and Warwick shook it firmly.

"Happy to help. It ain't every day an opportunity like this comes up. And when you see your uncle, punch him for me, would ya?"

A huge smile came to my lips. "Absolutely."

We had been walking for an hour according to the position of the moon, when we had to stop and rest. I sat on a fallen log, took water out of my pack and drank furiously. Sam and Melissa did the same. Nightshade, however, stared at the map, his brow furrowed.

"Anything interesting?" I asked.

Nightshade shook his head. "It should be right around here, but I do not understand why we are not finding it."

"Warwick said the glade would show itself when it wanted to," Sam reminded him.

"You mean like that?" Melissa pointed past me, and I swiveled my body around.

About a hundred yards away, a thicket of pine trees glowed like someone had dipped their branches in a vat of radioactive glitter. We all looked at each other and smiled.

Nightshade rolled up the map, and we ran to the glade. We stopped at the opening and stared at the beautiful woman standing before us. Her skin was almost translucent, with an ethereal glow. Her long, white hair flowed down to her waist in perfect curls, and she was wearing a pure white dress that seemed to dance with the light of a thousand stars.

"My name is Solara," the woman said. "I am the Protector of the Glade of the Hanged Man, and I've been expecting you for a long time."

I stood in front of Solara in stunned silence. She'd been expecting me? What did that mean? I opened my mouth to ask, but Solara merely raised a hand to silence me.

"There is no time for questions. Your quest is noble and I will help you. Please hand me the map." She held out her hand expectantly.

"You know of our quest?" I asked.

Solara nodded. "Yes, and I expect you have many questions, but now is not the right moment for answers. Time is of the essence."

I nodded at Nightshade. He placed the map in Solara's outstretched hand. As soon as the parchment touched Solara, it glowed. She handed it back to me and the scribbles written all along the edge of the map changed into decipherable words.

"The key to the map was you." Sam said, mystified.

We looked down at the map to read the riddle.

"These words are just directions," I said as I looked up, but Solara and the glade were gone.

"Wicked cool," Sam said.

We were about halfway to the old ruins, according to Nightshade, when Sam twisted his ankle in a hole.

We sat down under the canopy of the forest and tended to his ankle. Nightshade gave Sam a salve to help with the pain, but it needed a few minutes to work. So we sat and listened to the sounds of the forest. The chirps of the crickets were especially clear, and an owl hooted in the distance. Fall in Amethystia wasn't as cold as autumn in the human realm, so we didn't need a fire. When Sam said he couldn't feel the pain anymore, we continued our journey.

The rising sun silhouetted the castle ruins against a pink and purple sky. They were massive. Bigger than our palace. We stopped at the entrance and ogled. The walls crumbled as nature reclaimed the castle, but it must have been something in its time. Nightshade said there was a body of water to the west, so we followed the castle wall until we found the Onyx Sea.

We gawked at the expansive body of water. No way were we going to find the cavern. Nightshade saw the doubt on my face and squeezed my shoulder.

He bent down, letting his breath caress me and whispered, "You can do this."

That was all the encouragement I needed. I closed my eyes and took a deep breath. The sword had a hold on me. I reached out with my body and my mind. Nothing. I opened my eyes and sighed. That always worked in the movies. Everyone looked at me curiously and I shook my head.

"Maybe if you get in the water?" Melissa suggested.

"Worth a shot," I said.

I took off my shoes and walked into the surf. A jolt immediately ran through me and I turned to the right. I motioned my friends in.

"It's over there." I pointed to where I felt the pull.

"Sam can't swim with his ankle, so we'll stay here," Melissa said, holding Sam's weight.

"Are you sure?" I asked.

She nodded.

"Be careful," Nightshade warned. "And if you hear or see anything, hide."

"Will do." Melissa helped Sam hobble to a rock and sat down.

"I don't know how far the cavern is, but we can't swim the entire way there." I said to Nightshade.

"It looks like we do not have to."

He pointed about ten yards away at a rowboat tied to an old dock. It looked sturdy enough, but I wasn't so sure.

Nightshade carefully stepped into the boat. It held his weight. He held out his hands, and I took them. He helped me step into the boat and thankfully, it held both of us. We untied the boat from the dock and pushed off. Sam and Melissa watched us paddle away.

"This would be romantic if I wasn't afraid we'd drown any second," I said jokingly.

Nightshade chuckled. "I will take you on a real romantic boat ride someday."

"Promise?"

"Promise."

When we reached the spot the sword had pulled me to, we stopped. We were in the middle of the sea with nothing around us.

"Are you sure this is right?" Nightshade asked.

I nodded. I stuck my hand in the water and the shock was so bad I thought I would overturn the boat.

"About four hundred feet down, there's a cave," I said.

"Then let us get swimming," Nightshade said.

Nightshade handed me some loglea, an herb that helps you breathe underwater while I performed a spell to keep the water pressure from crushing us. The water was freezing cold as we made our way down to the cave. We found the entrance about fifteen minutes later. Nightshade went in first, and I followed.

We emerged in the middle of an enormous cavern. Nightshade got out of the water and helped me up onto the slippery surface of the rocks.

I was soaked. My hair dripped onto my face, and my clothes sloshed with every movement. My lips quivered as the cold from the cave seeped into my skin. Nightshade looked like he wanted to help, but I brushed him off. We didn't have the time.

"*Illuminare.*" I whispered.

A ball of light shot out of my hand and hovered about five feet in front of us, guiding our way. We walked for a couple miles when we came to two caves branching off in either direction.

"Wh-which way d-do we g-go?" I asked, shivering.

Nightshade looked just about as miserable as I was with long hair sticking to his body and his lips quivering. I wanted to help him just as badly as he wanted to help me.

He shook his head. "I do not know. Can you feel anything?" He struggled to sound normal.

"Not when I'm this c-cold," I said.

We chose the right tunnel. It sloped downhill and the moss growing on the rocks did little to help my stability. I slid all over the place, and Nightshade didn't fare much better. He offered to help me keep my balance and I accepted just so I could be closer to him.

The tunnel narrowed until we had to walk single file. I had never felt claustrophobic, but the bumpy walls closed in around me.

The tunnel finally opened up to a large room with more tunnels extending in all directions. Nightshade and I entered the room and examined it. Stalactites hung from the ceiling ominously, almost as if they were teeth waiting to chew us to bits.

We stood in the middle of the room and Nightshade directed me to feel the pull of the sword. I was shivering so hard I could barely concentrate, but I did what he asked. I closed my eyes and Nightshade led me around the room. Grunting in frustration, I opened my eyes. It was no use. My body's dropping temperature obstructed my ability to tell if we were close to the sword.

"Concentrate," Nightshade said.

"I'm trying!" I shouted. The echo was immediate.

"Maybe this will help."

He wrapped his arms around me from behind and held my body close to his. His plan to warm me up with his body heat was working. I leaned into him and sighed. Even though his clothes were as wet as mine, and he was probably just as cold as I was, his body was warm and inviting.

I closed my eyes again and this time I felt a slight tug at the tunnel in the middle.

"That one," I said, pointing.

"Good," he whispered and kissed my neck. I shivered again, but it wasn't from the cold this time.

We explored the middle tunnel for a while before we came to another large room. It had no tunnels, and the sword was nowhere to be found. We had hit a dead end. I looked around the room and groaned. Nightshade held my hand and squeezed tightly. He could tell I was frustrated. I squeezed his hand back as I closed my eyes and concentrated really hard. The pull of the sword felt stronger here, and I walked toward the wall on the right.

I didn't know how I knew, but there was a door there. A hidden door. I just needed to find the way to open it.

I told Nightshade what I found, and we searched the area, looking for any sort of lever or button. We didn't find any, and I sat down, my back sliding against the wall.

"Maybe they protected it with a spell," he said.

"That could be, but what spell?"

Nightshade turned thoughtful. He sat beside me and put his arm around my shoulders and pulled me against him. I scooted closer.

I closed my eyes and let myself have a moment of peace. I listened to the sound of dripping water from the stalactites above us.

A whispering made its way into my ears.

"Did you say something?" I asked Nightshade.

"No."

I listened for the whispering again. It was barely there at first, but then it grew louder and louder.

Eventually, I had to cover my ears to muffle the sound. Nightshade looked at me worriedly.

"Are you having another vision?" he asked.

I could barely hear him, but I shook my head. I stood and faced the hidden door, then put my hand against an oddly shaped stone on the wall.

"*Revele ostium absconditum.*"

The door disappeared in a golden mist, revealing a passage that hadn't been there before. The whispers faded, leaving me in silence once again.

"How did you do that?" Nightshade asked.

"I don't know, but let's not waste any more time." I headed through the opening.

Nightshade followed closely behind. Torches flared as we passed, making the tunnel bright and, more importantly, warm. I extinguished the ball of the light in front of us. We wouldn't need it anymore.

The tunnel opened into another large room, but this time, the room wasn't empty.

Torches lined the walls all around us, and an altar stood in the middle of the room. On the altar were several candles and a long golden box. The pull of the sword was so strong I could barely focus, but I managed to tell Nightshade that the sword was here.

We carefully walked up to the altar and Nightshade felt around for any protection charms.

"There are at least five different spells on this altar." Nightshade ran his hands through his drenched hair in frustration.

"Great. Any idea how we get around them?" I clenched my jaw.

He shook his head. We were so close, and yet so far.

I closed my eyes and begged the sword for another sign. Of course, no sign came, and I felt stupid asking a sword for help.

Nightshade roamed around the chamber, inspecting everything from the torches to the tapestries on the walls.

Sounds came from the tunnel and Nightshade and I looked at each other. There was nowhere to hide, so he rushed to my side and took out his blade. I put my hands in an offensive position, and while the torches warmed up the room, my hands trembled from the cold. I didn't think I was going to be much help in a fight.

Shadows danced across the floor as three creatures just like the ones that attacked Fabian and me trudged into the chamber, brandishing bulky clubs.

CHAPTER NINETEEN

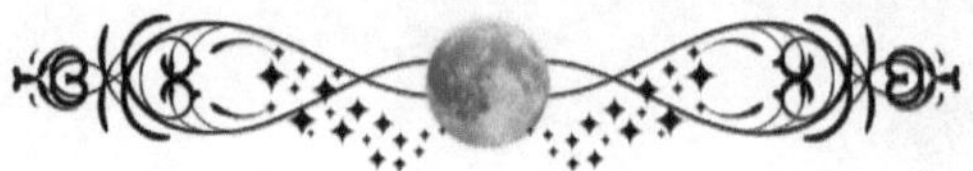

"WHO ARE YOU? HOW did you get in here?" one of the creatures said in a raspy voice.

Nightshade stepped forward. "I am Nightshade Oakenheart of the Regelves and this is Ebony Amberwood of the Amberwood family. We are here looking for the sword of the Delacroix family."

"Amberwood?" the creature rasped. "What does an Amberwood want with the sword?"

"Something bad is going to happen tomorrow. The sword can help us stop it," I said, stepping next to Nightshade.

"Yes, we have heard about the calamity that is going to take place. We will watch with enjoyment," another of the other creatures said.

The first creature lumbered toward me. I tensed. It squinted its yellow eyes at me and stared for a long time. The creature backed off and smiled, showing jagged teeth.

"I am Ar'gath, leader of the Bogromoks and protector of the sword of the Delacroix family. You are welcome here."

"Thanks," I said and cautiously lowered my arms.

"We need to take the sword with us." Nightshade said, sheathing his sword reluctantly. "But the protection charms on it are extraordinarily powerful. We cannot break them. Would you be able to?"

"We would," Ar'gath said.

"Are you going to?" I asked when they didn't move.

"No," it said. "You must do something for us first."

"What is it you want?" Nightshade asked warily.

"Her blood."

The two creatures behind Ar'gath laughed, and Nightshade immediately moved in front of me.

"No," he said harshly, resting his hand on the pommel of his sword.

"Then we will not help you."

"How much blood do you want?" I asked, stepping around Nightshade.

"All of it," one of the other creatures bared its yellow teeth.

"Just a vial," Ar'gath corrected.

"What will you do with it?" Nightshade asked.

"That is none of your concern," it answered.

"I'll do it," I said.

Nightshade looked at me like I was deranged. And maybe I was, but we didn't have time to argue. Besides, my blood wasn't special.

I held out my arm. "Go ahead."

All three creatures laughed, and Ar'gath sliced my palm open with their claw. I winced.

It produced a small vial (from I didn't want to know where) and held it under my hand. I tilted my hand so the blood flowed into the glass. When it was full, Ar'gath corked the vial and Nightshade helped me bandage the wound.

"Excellent," it said.

"Now, will you take down the protection charms?" I asked impatiently.

"No," it said.

"You lied." I conjured a fireball and was about to heave it at them.

"We cannot break the charms," it said. "but you can. Just a drop of blood over the box is all you need."

"Why did you not tell us that in the first place?" Nightshade asked through gritted teeth.

"We wanted the blood," one of the Bogromoks standing by the passageway said.

"Of course you did," I muttered.

I stood over the altar, unbandaged my hand, and a drop of blood fell as I clenched my fist over the box. I lowered my arm and Nightshade checked for the protection charms.

"They are gone," he said, mystified. "How did you know—"

Nightshade turned around to ask the Bogromoks his question, but they were gone.

I carefully clasped the box. The pull of the sword was so strong it was almost nauseating. Nightshade put his hand on one of mine.

"It's okay," I told him, though I was grateful for his support.

He removed his hand, and I cautiously opened the lid. The sword glowed brightly in its velvet lined case. I caressed the air above the sword. The magic coming off it was astonishing. It looked just like it did in my vision. The grip was made of worn brown leather. The pommel was a glittering ruby, and the blade was made of aged Igarate, a metal so black it barely looked real. I glanced at Nightshade, who stared at the sword with a mixture of awe and fear. I couldn't understand the fear on his face, but the awe I understood. Looking at this sword was like looking at a majestic creature.

"We have the sword. We should get back," Nightshade whispered.

I nodded, but what he said didn't really sink in. My hand lowered to grab the sword, but Nightshade gripped my wrist.

"Leave it in the box," he said.

I took one more wistful glance at the sword before shutting the lid. Once the sword was out of my sight, I could think more clearly. I shook my head, trying to relieve the stupor, and stuffed the box into my bag. It wouldn't fit all the way, but it fit enough to get it to the surface.

We retraced our steps, and found the pool of water that led to the sea.

"Ready to go swimming again?" he asked in a lighthearted tone.

I groaned and shook my head. Nightshade chuckled, and like he did on the surface, he splashed into the water first and helped me in after him.

We returned to the surface, and our boat was right where we anchored it. Nightshade scrambled into the boat and steadied it for me. I tossed the bag with the sword in first and I climbed up after.

We docked the boat next to the ruins, and Melissa and Sam ran over to us.

"Did you get it?" Sam asked.

I showed them my bag and nodded with a smile.

"Then let's go. We still have half a day's walk ahead of us," he said.

We headed back east toward the castle, but we didn't get very far before low growls erupted from the trees and four large Jaramoths surrounded us. They herded us tightly together. One of them howled, and the hooded figure emerged from the shadows.

"Thank you for finding the sword for me, Ebony. Now, if you'll kindly hand it over, I *might* spare your lives."

"As if we would hand anything over to you," Melissa spat.

The hooded figure laughed and flicked his hand. Melissa's arms twisted unnaturally, and the bones snapped sickeningly. She screamed in agony and dropped to the ground.

"Stop it!" I readied my magic.

"Hand over the sword."

"No."

The hooded figure shrugged and flicked his hand again. This time it was Sam who screamed in pain when his leg cracked.

"I said stop it!"

"One last time. Hand. Over. The. Sword."

Nightshade put his hand on my shoulder and gave me a resigned look. They outnumbered and outmatched us. I tried to protest, but he silently shook his head. My shoulders sagged. Did we really go through all of that just to have our prize ripped away? Sam and Melissa clung to each other, trying to ease each other's pain. I looked back at Nightshade and nodded. Turning toward the hooded figure, I took the bag off my shoulders and tossed it at him.

"Thank you," he said.

I wanted to rip his head off. If he had one. The hooded figure disappeared into the shadows, just like he had emerged. The creatures backed off and ran after their master.

I sank down to help Sam and Melissa, but they looked at each other in confusion.

"I don't hurt anymore." Melissa tested her arms.

"Neither do I." Sam ran his hand over his leg.

Nightshade hissed. "An illusion spell. I should have guessed."

I helped my friends stand. "We need to get the sword back."

"How?" he asked in a clipped tone.

"I don't know. We'll think of something."

Nightshade just scoffed and stomped toward my family's castle.

We had very little trouble on the way back. Monsters and bandits seemed tosense our desolate mood, and they stayed away.

It was well after nightfall when we returned to the castle. Uncle Hesperus and my parents waited in the throne room. The fireplace blazed, and I was grateful. My clothes had dried on the journey home, but I was still chilled.

Nightshade, Sam, Melissa, and I sat around the fireplace while my parents stood on either side of my uncle's throne.

"Did you have any luck?" Uncle Hesperus asked.

"We found the sword." I couldn't look my uncle in the eye. I felt numb, and it wasn't from the chill I still had.

"That's great news!"

Nightshade stood up and faced my uncle. "We found the sword, but it is now in the hands of the enemy. I take full responsibility." He bowed his head and sat back down.

"Ebony, is this true?" Uncle Hesperus asked, horrified.

"It's true that the hooded figure has the sword, but it's my fault he got it, not Nightshade's." I warmed my hands and refused to meet his gaze.

"Then we are all doomed." Uncle Hesperus slumped in his throne. "Get out of my sight. All of you. I need to think."

We slowly got to our feet, and slogged out of the room.

"Once again, you have disappointed us, Ebony," my father said as the door shut behind us, making me feel like a failure once again.

Nightshade returned to the servants' quarters while Melissa, Sam, and I plodded to my room. We sat on my bed and talked. Melissa tried not to cry and Sam stared down at his hands.

"So, how did you find the sword?" Melissa cleared her throat.

I recounted the journey through the cave with Nightshade.

"How romantic," Melissa said when I got to the part about Nightshade helping me find the hidden passageway.

"Yeah," Sam agreed sullenly.

"What's up with you?" Melissa asked him.

Sam jumped off the bed. "They found the sword. Woo-hoo. But it's gone now and I, for one, would like to make a plan to get it back before my home—my family—dies."

"We will." Melissa rose from the bed and took Sam's hand.

He shook her off and left the room, slamming the door behind him. Melissa stared at the door longingly.

"He's just tired. We all are," I said.

"I know, but I thought maybe we were... that we were..."

"You are. He'll come around."

"You think so?" she asked between sniffles.

"I know so. We should get to bed. We have a big doomsday tomorrow."

Melissa nodded but made no attempt to move.

"You okay?" I asked.

She shook her head, her eyes hollow. "Tomorrow is it. The end of the world. The end of *both* worlds."

I stared at my hands fidgeting in my lap. "We'll stop it."

"I don't think we will. The sword was supposed to help stop doomsday, but we failed."

"We didn't fail," I said, not looking up from my hands.

She whirled toward me. Her face was blotchy and her eyes were wide and red from tears. "Yes, we did! We failed, and the world is going to end because of us!"

"We did not fail!" I shouted back at her. "We found the sword. We just—we just temporarily lost it. That's all. We'll get it back."

"There's no time to get it back."

"We'll get it back!"

A sob broke through my chest. My lungs constricted. Tears started pouring down, and I didn't even bother wiping them away. She was right. Uncle Hesperus was right. We failed and now we're doomed. All because of me.

Melissa's tears were streaming down in droves. She ran out the door, leaving me to break down in peace.

CHAPTER TWENTY

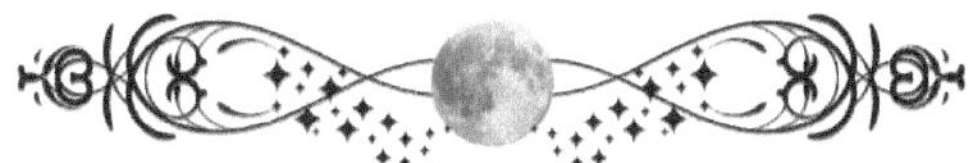

IT WAS HOURS BEFORE the tears finally stopped. The door to my room opened, and I sat up and sniffled.

Nightshade walked in and he handed me a cup. From the smell of the valerian and basil, I guessed it was his people's calming remedy. I sipped it gratefully.

"Are you all right?" he asked.

I shook my head. "We lost."

Nightshade smiled and smoothed my hair back. "How can we lose a fight that has not started?"

"We don't have the sword."

"So? We did not even know where the sword was until a couple of days ago. We still have a chance."

"You were mad," I said.

"I was. I was mad at myself for letting you and your family down."

"You didn't let us down. I let us down."

"You did what you thought was right."

I took another sip. I didn't know what our next move was going to be. Hell, I didn't even know if we would have a chance at making another move, but I wouldn't let my friends or my family get hurt. Not because of some faceless monster, and certainly not because of me.

Nightshade kissed the top of my head and ran his hands over my arms to soothe me. My eyes drooped. He took the cup from my hands and set it on my bedside table. I lay down, and he tucked me in.

"Nightshade?"

"Hm?" he said while still stroking his hand up and down my arm.

"Stay with me tonight."

He climbed into bed with me and cradled me in his arms until we fell asleep.

Bright light woke me the next morning. I groaned and squinted at the light. A servant had drawn the curtains. I shooed them away— I did not miss that part of being home. Nightshade stirred beside me, and I watched him wake up. He looked cute with his ears pointing through his long, messy lavender hair. He opened his eyes, and they were unfocused. Groggy. I giggled as he took in his surroundings.

"Good morning." I snuggled closer to him.

"Good morning." He kissed the top of my head. "Ready to face the end of the world?"

"No, but I will, as long as you're there with me."

"I will always be with you."

Nightshade left to change, and I examined my closet. I had forgotten how much leather I owned. I grabbed a gray cami and a purple sleeveless jacket, my favorite leather pants, boots, and arm wraps. If today was truly the end of the world, then I was going out in style.

I left my room and immediately ran in to Sam and Melissa.

"Hey," I said.

"Hey," they replied

We stood there for an awkward amount of time before Sam chimed in.

"I'm sorry to both of you for last night. I was tired, and—"

"And I'm sorry too," Melissa said. "All the pressure got to me—"

"No, I'm sorry," I said. "I dragged you both into this and you have been so amazing throughout this mess. I love you both."

"I love you both, too," Sam said.

"Same here." Melissa agreed.

The breakfast bell rang, and we giggled as we made our way to the great hall.

"I saw Nightshade sneak out of your room this morning." Melissa said in a scandalous tone.

"Nothing happened," I assured her. "We just slept."

"Uh-huh. Sure."

We opened the door to the great hall and the only people there were my family. Weird. Breakfast is usually the busiest time.

"What's going on? Where is everybody?" I asked as we took our seats at the family table.

"Everyone is preparing for the worst," Uncle Hesperus said gravely.

The chefs brought out our breakfast, and that thankfully ended the conversation as we dug into our eggs and ham.

"Ebony." My father called for my attention when my plate was almost empty.

"Yeah?"

"How long have you and that boy been sleeping together?"

I choked on the water I was sipping and my face heated.

"We're not—I mean he and I haven't—"

"A servant saw you two in bed together."

Damn that servant.

"It wasn't like that," I protested.

"You think because the realm might get destroyed, that gives you a right to behave like... like... that? We still have a family name to uphold."

"Are you mad because I had a boy in my bed or are you mad because he's the help?" I shot at Dad.

He's never liked me flirting with people we employed. He thought it was beneath us.

"How dare you!" His eyes bugged out.

"No, how dare you. I have busted my butt these past few weeks trying to save our home—my home. A witch hunter has hunted me, the ugliest creatures have attacked me, and I went in search of a mythical sword that no one even knew existed. What have you done?" I slammed my water down, spilling it, got up from the table, and left.

I ended up in my favorite place. The shimmering reflection of the water danced across the walls of the garden. It was mesmerizing. I sat on the edge of the pool and took my boots off. I dipped my feet in the refreshing water and took a deep breath.

I heard someone come in, but I didn't care. Whoever it was could go away.

Aunt Jasmine sat down beside me and crossed her legs.

I didn't even acknowledge her.

She sighed and nudged me. I nudged her back. She chuckled and I smiled.

"I want to go home," I said.

"You are home."

I shook my head. This wasn't home anymore.

Aunt Jasmine lifted her head up and gazed at the ceiling.

"I forgot how beautiful it was here."

"It's beautiful in the human realm, too," I said.

"Yes, it is, but in a different way."

Aunt Jasmine looked back at me and patted my knee. She got up and kissed the top of my head.

"It will all turn out fine. I'm sure of it." She walked out of the garden, leaving me alone once again.

I didn't know how long I had been in the garden. I just watched the shimmer of the water and smelled the aroma of the flowers, thinking about how everything got so twisted. My eyes sagged, but they popped open when someone slammed the door open and rushed in.

"Ebony!" Melissa yelled.

"What is it?" I asked, alarmed, leaping out of the water and standing up.

"The sky. It's darkening."

My heart skipped a beat. Doomsday wasn't supposed to happen until tonight. I quickly put on my boots, and Melissa and I rushed upstairs and out into the courtyard.

She was right. Dark clouds started rolling in from the east, and the air currents carried a feeling of dread with them.

"What do we do?" Melissa asked.

"I don't know," I said.

I grabbed Melissa's hand, and we ran back into the castle. I headed straight for the throne room. My uncle and all his advisors were speaking in strained voices.

"What's going on?" I asked.

"A servant found this tacked to your door." Uncle Hesperus handed me a piece of parchment that read in decadent handwriting: *Delacroix family castle. Sundown.*

"Done. I'll be there at sundown," I said

"It's not that simple." Dad said. "It's most likely a trap."

"Yeah. So, we set our own trap for the trap."

"And what do you propose we do for this reverse trap?" Uncle Hesperus asked.

"I haven't gotten that far yet." Several ideas popped into my head, but all of them were too risky, and would most likely get someone I cared about hurt.

"Well, when you're through wasting our time, we have a serious matter to attend to," one of the other advisors said.

"Ebony should go to the castle alone," Nightshade chimed in. I hadn't even noticed he was in the room.

"Not going to happen." My father stalked up to Nightshade and got in his face.

"Obviously, I do not mean she should actually go alone. Just make it look like she is."

"And then what?" Dad asked impatiently.

"When the hooded figure shows up, the guard ambushes him."

"That's not a bad idea," one advisor said.

"That could work," another one said.

The advisors soon filled the entire room, talking to one another, making plans, and shooting other advisors' plans down. Uncle Hesperus called for quiet, and the voices stopped.

"I'm not using my niece as bait. And that's final."

"What if I want to do it?" I needed to do this, needed to redeem myself.

I made so many mistakes over the past month. The sword, Sam getting hurt, Richelle dying.

"Ebony, please, now is not the time to play a martyr."

"It could work. Just let me try," I pleaded.

"And if this hooded figure captures you and uses you as a hostage?" my dad asked. "What then?"

I thought about it for a minute. He was right. What if I got captured? Would I be willing to risk everything just so we could catch the hooded figure? My dad looked smug when I hesitated, and I knew my answer.

"Leave me," I said simply.

"What?" My dad flinched and his face went pale.

"Leave me," I repeated forcefully. "If the hooded figure captures me, don't come for me. Just take him down."

"You do not know what you are saying." Nightshade stepped toward me.

I turned and faced him. "This was your idea."

"I did not mean risk your life."

He looked absolutely horrified at the thought of me putting myself in danger. I walked up to him and I kissed him. In front of everyone.

"I want to do this. Please let me do this," I whispered against his lips.

His arms wrapped around me, and he pulled me to him tightly.

"I cannot lose you," he whispered in an agonizing voice.

"I love you," was all I said in return.

I broke away from his embrace, his hands reluctantly letting me go, and marched up to my uncle.

"I'm ready to do this if you are."

Uncle Hesperus nodded, and preparations began immediately.

We didn't have time for a half-day hike, so Uncle Hesperus used his powers and opened a portal to the Delacroix family castle ruins. My family and I decided we all would go, plus a few guards. Melissa and Sam would stay at the castle, which they were not happy about.

"We can help," Sam pleaded.

I gave him a big hug. "I'm sorry, but I can't put you in any more danger. Take care of Melissa."

I broke the hug and walked through the portal.

The ruins looked as they had when I had first seen them, but something felt different. Something felt off. I turned around as each of my family members walked through the portal. They all wore leather combat clothes with weapons at their sides.

Once Uncle Hesperus strode through the portal, decked out in his combat leathers and wearing an air of confidence, he closed it. Not quick enough, though. Two more figures appeared from the portal.

"Sam! Melissa!" I hissed as dread filled my body. "What are you two doing here?"

"You didn't think you'd leave us behind, did you?" Melissa asked.

"Not after everything we've been through," Sam added.

Uncle Hesperus closed the portal and sighed. "Nothing we can do about it now."

"Open another portal and send them back!" I shouted. "It's too dangerous."

"We do not have the time," Nightshade said, placing his hand on my shoulder. "I will make sure they are safe."

I looked into his beautiful lavender eyes and nodded. He would keep his word.

The whole family grouped up, while the guards found places to hide.

"Are you sure about this?" my mom asked me.

I straightened my back. "As sure as I can be."

Her face was ashen as she gave me a big hug and found a place to hide with her guards.

Dad gave me a squeeze on the shoulder, kissed my forehead, and followed her.

"I really don't like this," Aunt Jasmine said, looking up at the sky.

"It'll be alright," I said with so much confidence, you would have thought I actually felt that way.

"Don't make me regret saying yes to this plan," Uncle Hesperus's voice was stern, but his eyes softened.

He kissed the top of my head and led Aunt Jasmine to their hiding places.

I turned toward Sam and Melissa.

"You two should probably hide as well." I said.

"Not a chance." Sam grabbed my hand.

"What he said." Melissa took a hold of my other hand.

I smiled. I had the best friends in the world.

The sky swirled with black clouds and the air changed from off to just plain foul. A noise came from behind me, and Sam, Melissa, and I faced in it. A figure appeared out of the shadows, but this time without his hood.

CHAPTER TWENTY-ONE

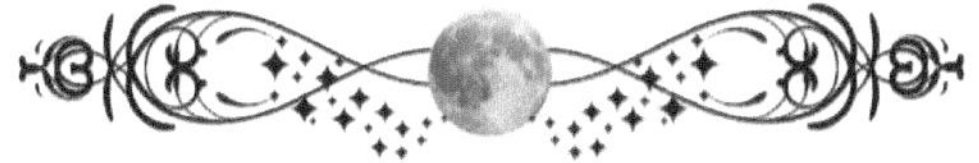

T HE FIGURE WALKED TOWARD us with the Delacroix family sword twirling in his hand.

"Fabian?" My mouth hung open, and I didn't think I could close it.

"Surprised?" he asked.

I regained some of my composure. I wasn't about to let Fabian get the better of me.

"A little," I said. *More like a lot.*

"I'm sure," he said with an arrogant quirk to his lips.

I wanted to wipe that smug, evil smile off his face.

"Sam. Melissa." He greeted my friends, who were the only things keeping me where I stood.

"Traitor," Sam said.

Fabian sighed. "While it is true I am a witch just like Ebony, I am no traitor. If anyone is the traitor, it's the entire Amberwood clan."

"What are you going on about?" I asked in a bored voice.

Fabian clenched his teeth. "You wouldn't know, would you?"

"I really don't," I said.

Fabian's mouth slackened and he blinked rapidly. Like he had expected me to gloat about whatever it was that he thought I did, but I hadn't.

"You really don't know?" he asked. He then broke into the most comically evil laugh I have ever heard.

"This is perfect!"

"Mind clueing us in, mister delusional?" Melissa asked.

Fabian stopped laughing. He looked at Melissa and Sam and waved his arm. They flew back into the bushes.

"Sam! Melissa!" I lunged toward where he threw them.

"Don't worry about them," His voice was closer than before. I whirled around and jumped. Fabian was right in front of me.

"If you hurt them..." I warned.

"You'll do what?" he sneered. "Kiss me? Like before?"

"I wouldn't kiss you again if you paid me."

Fabian grabbed my face roughly and smooshed his lips to mine. I tried to wiggle away, but he held fast. When the kiss broke, I almost gagged.

"Let your boyfriend think about that the next time he kisses you," he whispered.

I recoiled and my mouth dried up. He knew. He knew about our plan. I wrenched myself out of his grasp and turned toward the bushes. I was going to yell for everyone to get away, but it was too late. The Jaramoths had sniffed them out, and herded them toward us.

"I'm sorry," I whispered to Nightshade as one of the Jaramoths nudged him forward. He wouldn't look me in the eye.

The demons had herded my entire family out of their hiding spots.

"Where are the guards?" I asked.

"My pets had an early dinner," Fabian explained.

The blood left my face. I saw spots in my vision and they weren't from a premonition. What have I done? I led the guards to their deaths, and my family was now in the hands of my sort-of-hookup turned evil. My family stared at Fabian with disgust. All of them except my uncle, whose eyes were dull with resignation.

Sam and Melissa were the last ones to be herded out by the Jaramoths. Though battered from the fall, at least they were conscious. Fabian took one look at them and told the demons to back off.

"They aren't worth my time," he said.

Sam and Melissa held onto each other like they were each other's lifelines. I focused on them, begging them to run by sheer force of will. They didn't move. They just stood there watching Fabian drag us into his castle.

As he led us into the ruins, his demons made sure none of us tried anything. They herded us into the dungeon, the only part of the castle that looked like it had a makeover. They corralled us into one large cell, and the clang of the iron-barred door sealed our fate.

I raced up to the bars, thrust out my palm, and sent a blast of magic at Fabian. Or at least I tried to. Fabian laughed at the confused look on my face.

"These cells were meant to hold witches," he said. "You really think magic will work in here?"

"How about you come over here and I'll punch you in the face instead?"

Once again Fabian laughed. "Or," he suggested, "You could ask your family what is so special about your blood."

He pulled a vial out of his cloak. The dark red liquid sloshed around. I recognized it as the vial that Ar'gath had taken.

"Where did you get that?" I asked.

"I have friends in many places, which comes in handy when I need things like my enemy's blood. Or is it my family's blood? It gets so confusing. They're almost intertwined, just like us."

"We will never be intertwined. And what do you mean ask my family? They don't know anything."

"Oh, don't they? Ask why your aunt left. Why she *really* left."

I confronted my family. None of them would meet my eyes. Not even Aunt Jasmine.

"Aunt Jasmine," I said, "what's he talking about?"

"Your uncle found out about your mother's and my bloodline. Your bloodline." she said, still not meeting my eyes.

"What do you mean? What bloodline?"

Mom looked up at me with a grimace. "We had hoped you wouldn't find out, but I am a Delacroix. So is Jasmine. So are you."

"Only half." Dad said in a detached voice.

"It doesn't matter. Delacroix bloods runs through her veins." Mom put her hand on Dad's arm.

"So does Amberwood blood," Dad said fiercely.

"So... I'm both an Amberwood and a Delacroix?" I asked.

Mom nodded.

I turned back to Fabian. "What does that have to do with anything?" I yelled at him.

He stomped his foot like a petulant child. "It has to do with everything."

Movement behind him caught my eye.

"*I* was supposed to be the most powerful member of the Delacroix clan, and I was, until *you* came along. A witch with two of the most powerful bloodlines mixed together. I hated you for it. I wanted you dead."

Sam and Melissa tiptoed on either side of Fabian with swords they had picked up from the fallen guards.

"But then I had another idea. What if I were to seduce you? We could rule together, you and I. And it almost worked had it not been for your Regelf boyfriend."

"So, you want your power back?" I asked in a mocking tone, trying to give Sam and Melissa an opportunity to strike.

"Of course I do!"

"Then why not just kill me?" I smacked my hands against the metal bars, trying to keep his attention on me.

"You have no idea how powerful you —"

Sam and Melissa attacked. Fabian whirled around before Sam could swing the blade and thrust his hand out, blowing Sam back into the stone wall and knocking him out cold. Melissa, however, managed to swing the blade and lodge it in Fabian's shoulder. Fabian stumbled back screaming. He spun toward Melissa with a murderous glare. Fabian grabbed Melissa by the neck and hurled her into the bars of our cell.

"Melissa!" I cried. I tried to make sure she was alright, but Fabian grabbed her by the neck again and held her on display for my whole family to see.

"Well, well," Fabian said. "Looks like we have a hero. A *human* hero. Take a good look at what you've been trying to protect, because it's the last look you'll ever get!" Fabian tightened his grip on Melissa's neck and she cried out in pain.

"*Electricae!*" Fabian yelled.

Melissa's body convulsed from the shocks, and a few seconds later Fabian loosened his grip.

"No!" I screamed as Melissa's body slumped to the ground.

My body could no longer hold my weight, so I slid until I sat on the floor. Soundless sobs wracked my body. I looked over at Sam, who was still unconscious. I wanted to shout at him to wake up and make sure Melissa was okay. The truth was, I knew Melissa wasn't okay. The scorched skin around her neck in the shape of Fabian's hand proved that much.

Nightshade crawled over to me and tried to comfort me, but I shook him off. I didn't want to be comforted. I wanted to kill Fabian.

Fabian laughed as all of this happened, and I glared up at him furiously.

"You will regret the day you ever met me," I promised him.

"I regret the day you were born," he sneered. "Now sit back and watch as I destroy this world along with your precious human realm." He whistled at the Jaramoths to follow him as he disappeared into the shadows.

I sat on the cold, hard floor of the cell, staring at Melissa's lifeless body. Tears flowed down my face, and I sniffled so much I could no longer breathe.

Nightshade sat right beside me. He didn't touch me or try to comfort me. He just stayed by my side and watched me mourn the loss of my friend.

"Ebony." My mother tried to talk to me. I held up my hand for her to be silent. She was.

Sam stirred a while later and I quickly dried my eyes as best I could.

"Sam." My voice was hoarse. "Sam, wake up!"

He opened his eyes slowly and tested his body for any injuries.

"Ebony?"

"Yeah, it's me."

"Did we get him?"

I couldn't answer without sobbing again, so I didn't answer.

"Ebony," Sam tried again. "Did we get him?"

"No," I said, my voice cracking. "We didn't get him."

Sam sat up and took in his surroundings. He saw my tear-streaked face first. He looked confused, and then his eyes roamed to Melissa.

"No," he whispered. "No. No. No. No." He tried to stand, but his body wouldn't support his weight, so he crawled over to Melissa and shook her.

"Wake up!" he shouted. "Wake up!"

Tears pooled in his eyes, and a fresh wave of sobs broke through me.

"Why won't she wake up?" he asked.

All I could do was shake my head. Sam continued to shake Melissa, begging her to get up. She didn't. Sam's lips trembled, and he looked frail and broken. He spun toward me.

"Help her! Use your magic and help her."

"Magic doesn't work like that." Uncle Hesperus rubbed his hand down his arm. "Once someone is dead, that's it. They're dead."

"She's not dead!" Sam screamed, tears streaming down like waterfalls. "She can't be dead."

My chest was crushing me. I tried to take in a deep breath, but I couldn't. Melissa was dead. My best friend was gone.

Sam held Melissa in his arms, trying to get her to wake up for what seemed like hours. Finally, he gave up, hugged her to his chest and rocked her while he sobbed.

No one said a word. We just sat there, listening to Sam cry over the loss of his best friend.

Finally, Sam gently set Melissa down and stood up. I looked at him curiously. He grabbed a sword from the ground and prowled over to the cell. Nightshade and I backed up. Sam heaved the sword against the lock of the cell, breaking it open. The rest of us got up and clambered out of the cell.

"Thank you," I said, trying to give Sam a hug. He pointed the sword at me, and I froze.

"Don't come any closer," he said. "This is your fault. Melissa is dead because of you."

I was speechless. He was grieving, and he blamed me, but I didn't think he would hate me.

"Sam, I—"

"Don't."

"Okay." I raised my hands in a surrendering gesture.

"I'm going home, and I'm taking Melissa with me."

"I can't take you home, Sam. I don't have that kind of ability."

"But he does." He pointed the sword at my uncle.

"I will take you two home as soon as we finish this." Uncle Hesperus said.

"No. You'll take us home now."

I placed my hand on Uncle Hesperus's arm. "Take them home. This is my fight. No one else's."

"Ebony," my mother started.

"No, Mom," I said. "Fabian wants *me*. And I intend to give him just that."

My mom wrapped her arms around me. "I'm so proud of you."

With Sam's permission, Uncle Hesperus picked Melissa up.

"It will be easier to summon a portal in the throne room. The magic suppression down here is too strong," Uncle Hesperus said.

I snatched the other sword on the ground. Fabian's blood was all over it. Perfect. I followed the group only until we hit the stairs. My vision told me Fabian would be on the roof, so that's where I headed, too.

CHAPTER TWENTY-TWO

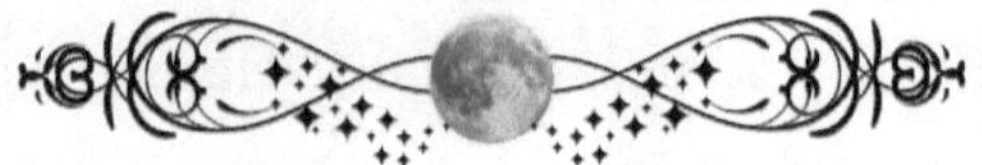

THE WIND HAD PICKED up, and the full moon was now a bloodred just like in my vision. I found Fabian on top of one of the towers. The Jaramoths blocked me as I raced over to him. I raised my sword, and they growled.

"You've angered my pets," Fabian said. "Put the sword down before you get hurt."

"You killed my best friend!" I yelled back. "You'll pay for that!"

The wind carried away Fabian's laugh.

"I very much doubt it."

Fabian jumped down from the tower and landed in front of me. I squared my shoulders and looked him straight in the eyes.

"I'm not scared of you," he said.

"According to you, I am the most powerful witch that has ever been born. You should fear me."

"Well then, a battle of magic," Fabian suggested. "No weapons."

"You want to duel me?" The last time I dueled, I was banished to the human realm. This time, I didn't care what my punishment was.

"Why not? It will be a fun way to end the world."

I bit back a retort and tossed the sword to the side. Fabian called off the demons, and they backed up, giving us some space.

I put my hands in an offensive position, and Fabian did the same.

"On my mark?" Fabian asked.

"On mine," I said through gritted teeth.

"Fine. On yours."

"Three. Two. O—"

Fabian blasted magic toward me. It sent me flying toward the edge of the roof. I recovered quickly and sent a blast of fire back toward him. He blocked it with a force field. I was stunned. I hadn't seen anyone put up a force field before. It was unheard of.

Fabian laughed and took advantage of my distraction. He sent a bolt of electricity toward me. It arced in the air, and I put my hands up to defend myself. The electricity didn't hit me. Instead, it bounced off an invisible wall in front of me. What the hell?

Fabian looked just as surprised as I felt. His face contorted into one of pure hatred and he tried to blast me with electricity once more. Again, it hit an invisible wall. There was a force field around me. Maybe there was something to being more powerful than I realized, even though I didn't know how I was doing any of this.

I wanted to mock Fabian, but he was already getting ready for his next attack. I readied my hands for an offensive move, and just as he sent yet another bolt of electricity toward me, I sent one right back at him. The two bolts hit, supercharging the air, and my hair rose from the static.

I didn't have time to react, though, because Fabian was already on the move. He ran for the tallest tower, and I rushed after him. Fabian climbed the dilapidated stones. No way could I follow him up there. Instead, I ran back to the edge of the roof, and I thrust my hand out, blasting the stone with magic. The stones around Fabian crumbled, and he fell to the ground. He rolled over and leaped to his feet. The glare he gave me sent chills down my spine and he yelled as he heaved a fireball my way. I raised my hands and hoped that the force field would protect me. The fireball struck my skin, and I screamed. My hands bubbled and smoked. I fell as dark circles encased my vision. Breathing grew difficult.

Fabian walked leisurely toward me, a smug look plastered on his face. He held the Delacroix sword. The reflection of the moon on the blade made something in the corner of my eye glitter. The sword I had dropped was laying nearly five feet away from me. I crawled backward in that direction, hoping Fabian didn't notice what I was after.

"I'm sorry it had to end this way." Fabian chuckled. "But as I suspected, you just couldn't match me."

He swung the sword overhead as I grabbed the hilt of the sword. He had just enough time to widen his eyes before the two blades clashed. Fabian was strong. Fire raced through my arm as my burnt hand protested my grip. I used my other hand to give myself more leverage. Fabian thrust his sword toward me, and I thrust my sword back toward him. I let go of the sword with one hand, giving Fabian some ground.

His face was close enough to touch. I grabbed his face and with a scream, I used all my strength to blast him away from me.

The Delacroix sword clattered to the ground as Fabian flew to the other edge of the roof, bellowing. He covered his face with his hand and got to his knees. Smoke rose from between his fingers. Though I only saw one of his eyes, the look he gave me was clear.

He was going to kill me.

I leaped to my feet and raced for the Delacroix sword.

Fabian pushed it away with his magic. I looked between him and the sword. Fabian was already getting to his feet. I raced toward Fabian, hoping to push him off the roof. He realized what I was doing, but I didn't care.

He grabbed any arms as I reached him, and he pivoted around, until I was the one on the edge. My feet dangled in midair. I held onto Fabian's arms for dear life, but he was stronger. He pulled my hands off him and I was free falling.

The ground raced toward me as the wind ripped away my scream.

I was about fifty feet from the ground when a spell popped into my head.

Without thinking, I yelled, "*Impetus tempestatis!*"

The wind strengthened and swirled in all directions, making my face raw, but it slowed my fall. My feet touched the earth softly, and once I was sure I was on solid ground, I started running.

I raced back up the steps to the roof, but by the time I got there, it was too late.

Fabian was on top of the tallest tower, the Delacroix sword raised high in the air. Black clouds swirled above his head and lightning struck the surrounding ground.

A slit in the sky appeared, and I heard menacing caws from the other side. I tried to approach Fabian, but lightning struck the ground in front of me. I looked around frantically for something that could help me and found nothing but crumbled rocks and the sword that Melissa had used to stab Fabian. My heart raced, and my breathing became shallow. I looked up at the sky and the slit widened, opening into a portal that would destroy both realms.

I was running out of time. I dashed toward the tower again, ignoring the lightning bolts as best I could. When I reached the side of the tower, I started climbing.

Huge, winged monsters poured out of the portal and flew in all directions. I kept climbing. I was almost to the top when I heard several cracks of thunder overhead. Another lightning bolt lit up the sky, only this time it didn't miss.

My body convulsed and my teeth rattled, but I held on to the tower for dear life. The lightning disappeared as soon as it came. I was alive. My back burned like the surface of the sun, but I was alive. I used that knowledge and kept climbing. I reached the top of the tower, and Fabian didn't even notice. He had his head to the sky and cackled like a madman. I used his distraction to my advantage, and I rushed him. I grabbed the hand that was holding the sword and used all my strength to pull his arm away from the portal.

"That fall should have killed you!" Fabian yelled.

"The lightning should've killed me. But I'm still here, you son of a bitch."

We grappled for the sword, neither of us giving an inch. He pushed me toward the edge of the tower, but I wasn't going to let him win. I used every ounce of strength I had and pushed him back. As I gained ground, his face contorted with more anger. I had him on the edge of the tower, above the Onyx Sea. He glanced behind him and looked back at me in fear.

"Please, Ebony. Don't do this. Don't kill me."

He sounded so scared. I let my strength wane and he smiled as he took advantage and grabbed the sword from my grasp. He sliced the blade against my face, and I yelped in pain as I stepped backward. I clenched my fist and gritted my teeth.

"Just like an Amberwood to be *cowardly,*" he said, spitting on the ground in front of me.

"I am an Amberwood." The sword hummed and it sounded like it was speaking to me, telling me its name. Like it didn't want to be used for destruction. "But I am also a Delacroix." I raised my hand and yelled, "Phantomseeker!" The sword glowed with a fierce light, and Fabian dropped it as if the sword had burned him. The sword flew into my hand and I pointed it at Fabian's throat.

"Call off the monsters," I commanded.

Fabian laughed. "So, the all-powerful Ebony Amberwood wants me to save her precious home. Not a chance, princess."

I thrust the sword a little closer to his neck, pushing him to the very edge of the tower.

"Do it. Or you die."

"You don't have the guts." He grabbed the sword with his hand, the blade cutting into his flesh.

I lowered the sword, and he laughed harder. I looked him straight in the eyes. He stopped laughing.

"Don't I?" I said as I hit him in the gut with the hilt of the sword, and he went tumbling over the edge, falling toward the rocky shore of the Onyx Sea.

I bit back tears as he fell to his death. This wasn't over, though. I took a step away from the edge and looked at the sky. The monsters were still pouring out of the portal by the hundreds. The sword hummed in my hand and pulsed with light.

Fabian had used the sword to open the portal. I thrust the sword high in the air. It did nothing.

"Close!" I shouted.

Still, nothing happened. A word popped into my head and the sword hummed louder.

I held the sword high above my head and shouted, "*Sigillum!*"

The sword pulsed with a light so bright I had to close my eyes. The monsters screeched as they reacted to the sword. Once the sword stopped humming, I opened my eyes.

The portal had vanished. The night sky was clear and the stars were more beautiful than I had ever seen them. I fell to my knees as I let go of the sword. It clattered to the ground as tears rolled down my cheeks. It was over.

I dried my tears and sheathed the sword before slowly—carefully—climbing down the tower. I entered the castle's throne room, but no one was there. Uncle Hesperus really took them all home. I took a deep breath, knowing everyone was safe, and I walked out of the castle, dragging the sword on the ground behind me.

CHAPTER TWENTY-THREE

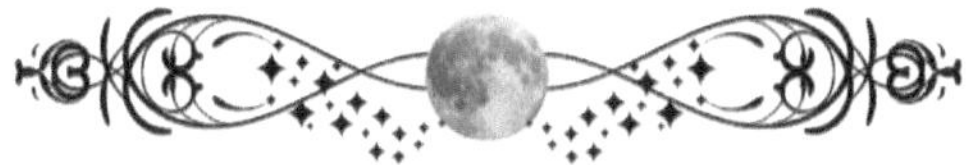

T HE SUN WAS PEAKING over the horizon as I made my way back into the central city. Smoke billowed from almost every building, and people cried through the street. I reached the castle entrance, and I stood—looking at the stone structure—like a fool.

"Ebony?" Nightshade called from the front door.

He didn't seem real. He rushed over to me and took me in his arms. My body tightened in pain, and he immediately let me go.

"Are you all right?" he asked. "What happened?"

I couldn't answer. All I saw was concern for me as I looked into his all too trusting eyes. I fell to the ground as sobs wracked my body.

"Ebony!" Nightshade cried.

He kneeled in front of me, trying to get my attention. When I wouldn't respond, he put his arms underneath my body and picked me up. He cradled me as he rushed inside. I didn't pay attention to where we were going. All I knew was that I was safe, and it was over. The sobs stopped as he rounded a corner and gently laid me down. I knew he didn't lay me down in my room, because this surface was too scratchy. It wasn't as comfortable as my bed. Still, it was comfortable enough for me to fall quickly into unconsciousness.

⟩ ⟩ ● ⟨ ⟨

I woke to the sound of whispering voices and a crackling fire. My body ached in pain as I tried to move.

"Do not move," a voice beside me said.

"Nightshade?" I croaked.

"I am here." He gently laid his hand on my forehead.

"What happened?"

"I was hoping you could tell me."

I recounted everything to the best of my ability, realizing I should have left certain parts out when Nightshade's face contorted with pain.

"Where's Sam?" I asked, wanting to change the subject.

"He... took Melissa home."

I nodded. Of course he did. At least Sam could rest, knowing that Fabian would never be a problem again.

I drew back the covers and started to sit up when Nightshade pushed me back down.

"What are you doing?" he asked.

"I need to talk to my uncle," I said, wincing every time I moved.

"Not now. For now, you rest." Nightshade gently pushed me back into a horizontal position and kissed my forehead.

I tilted my head up so that his lips connected with mine. Every synapse in my body was working overtime, and when we broke the kiss, I was breathing hard. Nightshade chuckled and kissed my forehead once more.

"Sleep now, my love."

I would have protested, but my body was already coming down from the kiss, and I drifted into unconsciousness once more.

$$) \cdot) \cdot \bullet \cdot (\cdot ($$

My eyes opened, and I looked around for Nightshade. He wasn't in the infirmary. No one was. I pushed myself out of the uncomfortable cot and made my way to the open window. It was night outside. It couldn't have been any later than one a.m. judging by the position of the moon.

My body was slow and stiff as I walked out of the infirmary, and I found my way to the throne room. Uncle Hesperus sat on his throne, his face leaning on his hand as his advisors bored him with something. My parents were also in the room listening, but they quickly turned their attention to me when I walked in.

"Ebony, thank goodness." Uncle Hesperus's body sagged. "How are you feeling?"

"Fine. What's going on?"

"We were deciding how best to handle the situation in the human realm," my dad said.

"Horus," my uncle warned.

"She should know." Dad helped me sit down.

"Know what?" I asked.

My uncle sighed. "Those creatures have devastated the human realm. They've leveled cities, and many people have died."

"What do we do?"

"We wanted to send one, maybe two, of our best to assess and fix the situation. The humans are terrified, and witch hunters are coming out of the woodwork," my dad said.

"Okay. Who are you sending in? I'll brief them about what to expect in the human world," I said, but truthfully, I didn't know what to expect there anymore.

"Well," my dad said thoughtfully, "we were thinking about sending Jasmine. And you."

I straightened in the chair, stunned. "Me? Why?"

"In case you haven't noticed, the only reason we're here right now is because of you," Uncle Hesperus said. Nightshade must have told them what happened.

"I-I did what anyone would have done."

"But it was *you* who did it," my dad said, coming to sit by me. "And I have never been more proud."

My cheeks went hot. My dad had never said he was proud of me before. I didn't know what to say, so I just smiled at him.

"And when you're done there, I want you to come back here and be one of my advisors." Uncle Hesperus clapped my back.

My mind went blank. Being an advisor to the king of Amethystia was a very important task. Mom sat on my other side and put her hand on my shoulder. I gently shook it off and stood up.

"Uncle Hes-Your Highness." I started, "thank you for the opportunity, but I would like to stay in the human realm."

Complete shock covered Uncle Hesperus's face. I had offended him, and I hoped it wasn't going to result in punishment.

After a moment, his face went from shocked to thoughtful to resigned.

"If you wish," he said. "But I ask that you take Nightshade with you. For your protection, of course."

I smiled widely. "Of course."

"Then it's settled. I will make preparations immediately."

Dawn broke as Aunt Jasmine, Nightshade, and I said our goodbyes to Amethystia. Mom was crying as she hugged me so tightly I winced, and I have never seen Dad look so proud. Uncle Hesperus and Aunt Jasmine even said goodbye to each other. Nightshade carried my stuff for me as we went through the portal and ended up in Aunt Jasmine's house. Nightshade heaved my stuff onto my bed, and without missing a beat, grabbed me around the waist and pulled me close.

"Welcome home," he said as he put his lips to mine.

"I love you," I said when we broke apart.

"I love you," he whispered back.

Nightshade and I went downstairs, and Aunt Jasmine turned the TV on to the local news. I stopped dead when I read the headline. It was about Melissa's death. The reporter said it had been a freak accident. They also said the memorial service was going to be held tomorrow morning.

"They don't believe that, do they?" I asked, my voice breaking.

Aunt Jasmine shook her head. "They're probably trying to quell the panic and handle the matter internally."

She turned off the TV and turned toward me. "It won't be easy fixing all of this."

"We have to do it, though."

She nodded in agreement.

We filled the rest of the day with protecting the house with charms and spells, and preparing for the chaos that would inevitably ensue when the witch hunters came looking for us.

That night, after Aunt Jasmine had thoroughly enchanted the house, she made Nightshade and me watch one of her favorite chick flicks. I yawned after about the first five minutes of it and fell asleep on Nightshade's shoulder.

He gently woke me the next morning. We were still in the living room, and Aunt Jasmine was nowhere to be seen.

"What time is it?" I asked groggily.

"It is time to get ready for the funeral," he said.

My heart clenched in my chest. Melissa's funeral. How could I face Sam after what had happened? He hated me. Would he tell everyone I was a witch? I had to be prepared for that possibility. I took a shaky breath and got dressed.

I looked in the mirror and sighed. Melissa would have known what to wear to these sorts of things. I had no clue. All I knew was that black was the appropriate color, so I dressed myself in a black peasant blouse and black skinny jeans. I put my hair back because Melissa once told me it looked good that way.

I went downstairs and Aunt Jasmine was making coffee in the kitchen. She wore a black blouse and slacks. She sleeked her hair back into her usual ponytail.

"You look nice," she commented while waiting for the coffee to brew.

"I didn't know what to wear," I admitted.

She opened her jewelry box on the kitchen table and handed me a triple moon pendant. Two crescent moons on opposite ends of a full moon.

The pendent shimmered with hundreds of tiny crystals as it moved.

"It's beautiful," I said.

"It belonged to the last Delacroix king. Our family."

"This is what the intruder was looking for, wasn't it?" I asked.

Aunt Jasmine nodded as she fastened it around my neck. The pendent sat heavy on my sternum. At that moment, I knew Fabian had trashed our home. Fabian who had caused so many problems. Fabian, who was now dead.

I smiled at her, but it didn't reach my eyes. I couldn't smile today. The world had lost an amazing soul.

)) ● ((

It was a cold, cloudy day, perfect for the event. I looked everywhere but at the casket sitting in front of me. It seemed like the entire school attended. A single tear fell down my cheek, and I quickly wiped it away. A lot of people loved Melissa.

The funeral itself was okay. Many people told stories about how much she cared about and loved other people. I wasn't planning on making a speech, but when her dad asked if anyone else would like to say a few words, my feet moved without me telling them to.

I stood in front of the crowd, and I felt several pairs of eyes glaring at me. I took a deep breath and spoke.

"Melissa—" My voice broke, and I almost burst into tears. I took a minute to compose myself and started again.

"Melissa was my best friend. When I first arrived here, I had nobody. I was bitter and angry, but Melissa saw through the façade, and she wanted to be my friend. At first, I hated her. I hated that she would come up to me before class every day and talk to me about trivial things. But then I got to know her, and she became one of my best friends." I had to stop because tears were spilling down my face. "She was always there," I started again. "No matter what I was going through, she stood by me. She was more than just my best friend, she was my sister. I never got to tell her that, and I'm sorry."

I bowed my head, embarrassed that I had cried in front of so many people, and returned to my seat. Nightshade put his arm around me and hugged me to him as tears kept flowing.

After the service was over, everyone went back to Melissa's house for the reception.

"It was a lovely service," I heard someone say to Melissa's dad.

"She would have loved it," someone else said.

My breath started getting shallower, and the room was getting hot, so I made my way out to the patio. Few people were out there, so it gave me room to breathe.

"Hey," Sam said, walking up to me.

"Hey," I said weakly.

"What you said at the service... it was nice."

"I meant every word."

"Yeah."

"Sam, I—"

"I don't want to hear it. I won't tell anyone what really happened, but you and I, we're no longer friends."

His words were harsh, but I knew he was still hurting, and I couldn't blame him. I nodded in acknowledgment.

"Also," he continued, "if you or your aunt or your boyfriend try anything—if you guys use any magic for *any* reason—I will kill you." He turned and walked away, leaving me gaping after him.

When Aunt Jasmine, Nightshade, and I returned home, I told them what Sam had said. Aunt Jasmine stressed we'd have to monitor him. That if he did ever try anything to harm us, or join the witch hunters, we would have to take him down. Nightshade promised he wouldn't give up on Sam and that he just needed time. I had to agree. Sam mourned the loss of his best friend, but Aunt Jasmine was also right. If he tried to hurt me or my family, I would have to do what was necessary. But could I hurt one of my best friends? I didn't know.

All I knew was that I had a job to do here, and no one was going to stop me from doing it.

Rate and Review on Amazon and Goodreads!

Scan for Of Witches and Ruin Playlist

ACKNOWLEDGMENTS

I want to first thank my amazing mom, for which this book would not have been possible. She has been my biggest supporter, from reading through the rough draft with all the typos, to hearing me talk about my book nonstop, to even helping me fund the publsihing of this book.

I also want to thank my found family. Kristin, who has been a critique partner, and the best friend I could ever have, even when it feels like the book is all I talk about. Drew, who has been the best moral support, and Cal, who has talked me through ideas, and frustrations.

I want to thank my wonderful therapist, McKenna, for always giving me hope and the ability to believe in myself even when things were at their bleakest.

Next I want to thank my editor, Emily for being patient with me as she worked through all of the typos and edits that come with a debut novel. She is truly the best editor ever.

And finally I want to thank Booktok, because you guys have given me so much support and I can't thank you enough for that.

ABOUT ME

Julie Caldwell resides in Oklahoma where she was born and raised with her little black cat Absynthe.

Julie has loved to read since she could remember and that translated into writing with her starting with poetry and quickly turning into full length novels.

Julie loves telling stories in any capacity and has loved the arts since she was a child. Photography has always been a second passion to her and she went to an arts high school to pursue that love.